THE INFLUENCER

FRANKIE BOW

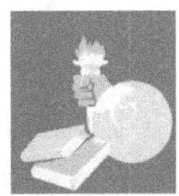

For those who are hoping to meet their heroes.
Please reconsider.

CHAPTER ONE

DR. EMMA NAKAMURA IS MY BEST FRIEND. WE BOTH TEACH AT Mahina State University in Mahina, Hawaii, where, according to our TV ads, "Your Future Begins Tomorrow." Over the years, we've come to know each other well. So I can tell right away when Emma is up to something.

Emma was trying to convince me she had dropped by my house for a cup of coffee because she "happened to be in the neighborhood." I knew better. In fact, she was angling to meet social media sensation Jandie Brand, who had recently moved into our new rental unit, separated from our main house by a mere quarter-acre of lawn. I'd tried explaining to Emma that Jandie and her husband had chosen our quiet street for the express purpose of avoiding pestering fans. Somehow Emma didn't think any of it applied to her.

Steadfastly ignoring Emma's increasingly-obvious hints, I opened the pantry to an eye-level stack of toilet paper and paper towels and a brickwork wall of blue Spam cans. A tropical storm was headed our way, so before Donnie left for the mainland, he had stocked us up on the essentials. I managed to dig out the coffee without knocking anything over.

"I knew I had a new box of coffee in here somewhere," I said. "Here we go. Mizuno Mart house brand."

"Maybe your tenants get some better coffee we could borrow," Emma said. "Let's go ask 'em."

"Seriously Emma?"

"What?"

Emma sat at my kitchen counter with an innocent look on her face. Looking innocent is easy for Emma. She's five foot nothing, with round, sun-freckled cheeks and wavy black hair pulled back in a casual ponytail. Thanks to all the canoe paddling she does, Emma is built like a very fit teddy bear. She also has tiny, childlike hands, something she hates having pointed out (I've had to learn this the hard way).

"Emma, you just told me you stopped by for a cup of coffee. Which is great, because I always like seeing you. This is the coffee I have. You want the coffee or not?"

"Yeah, Mizuno Mart coffee is fine. You're right, I didn't just come over to see you."

"A-ha! I knew it."

"My *schmendrick* brother is staying at my house. I needed a break."

Emma grew up just a few miles outside of Mahina, speaking Pidgin like everyone else around here. Then she went back east for grad school and picked up some Yiddish, which she uses frequently, mostly to enrich her insult repertoire.

"Jonah's at your house? Last I heard, he was living in Washington."

"He is. Guess it was too complicated for him to actually let me know in advance he was visiting. The first I heard of it was when he called me from the airport. I had to move out of the guest room so he could stay there."

"The guest room? Emma, why are you sleeping in the—know what, never mind, it's none of my business."

"No big deal, just Yoshi snores. It's like sleeping next to a running chainsaw. Or like when there's a hurricane and the

2

rain's coming down real hard on the metal roof. Oh, speaking of hurricanes, Molly I bet your tenants aren't prepared for the hurricane like you are. Maybe we should—"

"So we've made our way back around to my tenants now, have we? The hurricane is going to be down to a tropical storm by the time it hits us."

"Yeah, but do they know they're supposed to go out and buy extra toilet paper and Spam? I bet they don't. They're gonna starve to death, Molly, and it's gonna be our fault. Cause we didn't reach out an' help when we had a chance."

I finished brewing our two coffees and brought them over.

"Remarkable. Emma, I don't think I've ever seen you so starstruck before."

Emma snatched her coffee mug from me.

"I'm not starstruck. I just like following Jandie's feed and I think it's cool she moved to Mahina. To my best friend's house, even. What are the chances?"

"And you know why she came to Mahina, right? So she can take a break from her adoring public for six months."

"Molly, she doesn't need to be protected from me. I'm not one of her crazy fans. Know what I think? I think you just wanna keep her all to yourself."

Emma didn't actually say "so there!" but the way she drank her coffee implied it.

"Emma, I—"

"We should print out the hurricane checklist and bring it over. You don't want them getting swept away in a flood, do you?"

"We had the builders install steel foundation piers. No one's getting swept away."

"Molly, what is your problem, come on!"

"Look. Suppose we do walk over there. I'll say hey, you heard about the storm coming, here's the hurricane prep checklist, by the way, this is my friend Emma Nakamura,

3

everyone says oh nice to meet you, and then do we walk away like normal people?"

"That's right," Emma said.

"No, because then you'll just *happen* to mention how people are always telling you how much you look like Jandie and you'll make her stand there while you try to get a selfie with her—"

"Not." Emma crossed her arms and we glared at each other for a few seconds.

Finally, I said,

"Okay fine. But you have to give me your phone."

"Aw Molly, come on."

She handed me her phone in the end, because otherwise I would have refused to go at all. I printed out the Emergency Preparedness checklist from the County Civil Defense website, and Emma and I crossed the soggy lawn to the house next door.

I raised my hand to knock, but Emma stayed my hand. Someone inside was talking. Not Jandie. A man's voice.

"I think it's time to pull the trigger."

"How long?" said another man.

The voices lowered to a murmur.

"But that's what I'm trying to *saaaay!*"

Emma nudged me. We both recognized Jandie Brand's childlike voice.

"I'm not gonna bite the hand of the gift horse that feeds me."

"That's Jandie," Emma whispered.

"I know," I whispered back. "This is getting interesting."

"Okay, you two brain geniuses, riddle me this." This was Jandie again. "What about the landlady? She has a problem minding her own business. And she's kind of a crackpot, if you ask me."

"Hey," I mouthed. "*I'm* the landlady."

"Shh!" Emma shoved me.

"Now Jandie," said one of the male voices, "Ed's right. Know what they say, get it done now, you can always cry later."

I stood up straight and rapped the door. The conversation inside stopped dead.

"Someone's at the door," said the other man.

"Sorry, we're busy," Jandie shouted. "Can you come back later?"

"This is Molly from next door," I shouted back. "I brought over the hurricane checklist."

The door opened, and Edward Ladd stood there. I was struck by how far he was from his wife on the conventional-attractiveness scale. He was bald, beak-nosed, and older than Jandie by a generation or two.

I inwardly scolded myself for being superficial. Ladd must have a delightful personality. No, that, too, was a mean thought. *Try not to be so shallow, Molly.*

I cleared my throat and handed him the checklist.

"Hi. Hope you guys are doing okay. You've probably heard the weather reports. This is from the County Office of Civil Defense. In case you don't already have a copy."

"I'm Emma," said Emma.

"I can't have the power go out," he said as he looked it over. "Are you telling me I'm supposed to buy a generator now?"

"We've provided you a portable generator," I said. "It's in the carport. You can run your refrigerator, whatever else you need. Just don't try to use a microwave and a blow dryer at the same time."

"Where are we supposed to get two gallons of water per day?"

"The bottled water's going to be all sold out by now. Wipe out your bathtub with bleach, fill it up with water, and add another capful of bleach. It'll be safe to drink."

FRANKIE BOW

"Do you want us to show you guys how to use the generator?" Emma asked.

"No. We'll figure it out."

He closed the door without further niceties.

"What a *putz*," Emma remarked as we walked back up the grassy hill toward the road. "Totally blocked us. Not even a little peek."

"Maybe she asked him to keep people away. I told you they wanted privacy. Hey Emma, did you hear what Jandie said about me?"

"No one was talking about you."

"She called me a crackpot. Why would anyone say I'm a crackpot?"

"Molly, no one thinks you're a crackpot. Guarantee. I mean, you can be inflexible, obsessive, neurotic—"

"Thank you, Emma, I get it."

"Self-centered, kind of un-self-aware—"

"Yes, thank you, Emma. What are you OW!"

Emma was clutching my arm. It was pretty painful, to be honest. Emma has an alarmingly strong grip, especially considering how tiny her hands are.

And then I saw the cause of Emma's alarm.

"It's her," I stammered. "What's she doing here?"

CHAPTER TWO

STROLLING DOWN OUR SIDE OF UAKOKO STREET WAS A BLONDE woman in a long-sleeved muumuu. The two Yorkshire terriers she was walking had been groomed to look like silky mops. All three of them, the woman and the two Yorkies, wore matching yellow hibiscus flowers tucked behind their ears.

"I can't believe it," Emma said. "I thought Linda retired."

"She did," I replied. "Being retired just means you don't have to go to work, though. It doesn't turn you invisible."

Linda Wilson had been a higher-up in the Student Retention Office at Mahina State. Emma teaches introductory biology, which makes her the designated dream-crusher for aspiring health professionals. There was no way those two were ever going to see eye-to-eye. Because I was Emma's friend, Linda had always had it in for me too.

"Linda," I squeaked. "What a pleasant surprise!"

"What are you doing here?" Emma demanded.

"Molly, Emma, it's so nice to see you. Pele, Hiiaka, and I are just going for our daily walk."

The two leashes went taut as the Yorkies sprang at us with their teeth bared.

"How nice. That's exactly what we're doing too. Walking."

My reflex, even now, was to appease Linda by agreeing with whatever she said. "Gotta get those steps in, right? Look at us. What are the chances? All of us here, walking on Uakoko Street?"

Linda motioned us closer and I caught a whiff of cigarette smoke.

"Do you know who lives in that new ohana building?" Linda whispered to Emma. She was pointing to my rental unit. "Social media influencer Jandie Brand."

"Who?" I asked innocently.

"Oh, Molly." Linda shook a playful finger at me, rattling her gold bangles. "You think we're just little country bumpkins out here in Mahina. 'Who' indeed."

"No, I didn't mean—"

"Jandie Brand is actually very famous on the internet," Linda explained to Emma.

"That's great, Linda," Emma replied flatly.

"And Molly knows her better than any of us, don't you, Molly?"

"I don't interact with her much," I said. "I try to give them their privacy."

"Well, the next time you see Jandie, you can tell her I have a message for her."

"A message? Okay, no problem." I had zero intention of passing on any message from Linda Wilson. But Linda didn't need to know that.

"Tell her it's fine to post all the food and flowers and waterfalls, just like every other visitor to Mahina, but do you know what would really improve her feed? Some cuddly fur babies."

"Cuddly fur babies. Sure." I stepped back as the Yorkies lunged and snapped at my ankles.

"I know she would enjoy meeting Pele and Hiiaka. Everyone does. Molly, you *will* introduce us, won't you?"

"Umm…" I glanced at the sky, which had taken on an

8

ominous greenish cast. "Now isn't a good time with the storm coming. We're all battening down the hatches. In fact, we probably shouldn't even be out walking."

"Of course. Perhaps in a day or two, after the rains have passed," Linda said sweetly.

"Linda," I said, "please don't tell anyone Jandie's here. She and her husband value their privacy and the last thing she needs is to get swarmed by fans."

Linda said nothing, a stiff smile frozen on her face.

"I mean, I'm sure she would love to meet *you*, and your adorable...fur babies, of course. But please don't tell anyone *else*."

Linda unfroze.

"Yes, of course. I'll be in touch."

Linda continued to glide up the street in her long muumuu, her two little mop-dogs scampering angrily around her feet.

Emma and I rushed into the house. I shut the door behind us and locked it firmly.

"How did Linda find me?" I gasped. "And how on earth did she know about Jandie Brand?"

"Yeah, that was a bad surprise. I need a drink."

"Emma, it's ten in the morning."

"Bloody Mary it is. Where's your vodka?"

I sank onto my couch.

"On the counter next to the toaster. The bloody Mary mix is in the door of the fridge. Emma, Linda's going to blab to everyone about my having a celebrity tenant. People are going to come swarming around to harass them. This is exactly what I promised wouldn't happen."

"Unless you arrange an introduction for Linda and her little hellhounds." Emma plunked down next to me with a glass in each hand and handed me one. I took a cautious sip and quickly set the glass down.

"What is this, half vodka?"

"I would've put in more, but that's all there was in the bottle."

"What was Linda doing on my street? How did she know my personal business?"

"Are you seriously asking, Molly?"

"I know. It's Mahina. Everybody knows everyone's business. Of course Linda knew, somehow. Dangit."

"You should be used to it by now," Emma said. "Remember that time you was buying a whole bunch of booze and underwear at Galimba's Bargain Boyz an' it turned out the boy at the cash register was one of your students?"

"I had no reason to be embarrassed," I said. "Those were all perfectly legitimate purchases."

"Exactly! Who cares if everyone at Mahina State knows your exact bra size. Same thing when you was going to see the shrink—"

"I'm not sure this is helpful—"

"Oh yeah," Emma said, "and remember that thing with Stephen Park? Your students knew he was cheating on you before you did."

"Emma, what is your point?"

"I'm just giving you examples of how you can't expect to have any privacy in Mahina. So don't stress yourself out about it."

I chugged the remaining contents of my glass.

"There's seriously no more vodka?" I asked.

"Nope. We drank the last of it."

"It's not the privacy issue, Emma, it's the Linda Wilson issue. I thought when she retired that was it. I'd never have to deal with her again. And today she pops up right in front of my house with her snarling little 'fur babies'. Not what I needed right after overhearing my tenant complain about her nosy landlady."

"To be fair, Molly, you wouldn't have heard it in the first place if you hadn't been—"

"Oh, and I didn't even tell you, here's another layer on my spring break stress cake. Victor Santiago, the donor relations guy, wants my students' business plans featured at this year's Senior Showcase."

"Isn't that good?" Emma asked. "Senior Showcase is a big deal."

"No, not good. Because if my students' presentations are anything other than perfect and one hundred percent inoffensive, I'll be vilified for alienating our donors. And if everything is flawless and anodyne, I'll get in trouble for boring them. And if I refuse to participate, I'm not a team player. Emma, after the latest budget cuts, external donations are our lifeblood. I'm afraid I'm going to mess things up for everyone."

"You'll be fine, Molly. You got this. Didn't you just go to some donor dinner thing last year?"

"You mean the one where Donnie and I were forced to sit at the same table as my ex, I sprang a breast milk leak that ruined my favorite blouse, and oh yeah, *someone died*, and I got blamed for it? *That* donor dinner?"

Emma cleared her throat.

"Uh, no, I meant a different one. Eh, someone's at the door. I'll go see who it is. If it's Linda I'll tell her you left."

Emma ran over to the front door and pressed her eye to the peephole. The relief in her body language signaled it wasn't Linda.

My visitor was Mr. Henriques, my retired next-door neighbor. At least I assumed he was retired, based on the fact that he seemed to spend his days at home, observing the comings and goings of Uakoko Street.

"Eh Mr. Henriques," Emma said. "Nice to see you. Come in. You like some coffee?"

CHAPTER THREE

MR. HENRIQUES WAS ABOUT MY HEIGHT, WITH A MOON FACE and a few strands of black hair spread thinly over a large head. I couldn't help it: I found Mr. Henriques thoroughly annoying. I also felt guilty about this because I could tell he was lonely.

"Oh, hello Mrs. Nakamura. Mrs. Gonsalves. Just a glass of orange juice, please." He came in and sat on the couch cushion next to Emma. "What's the matter with the Ladds? They're making so much noise I cannot hear my shows."

"I don't have any orange juice," I said. "Did you say something is going on next door?"

He braced his hands on his knees and stood up.

"I like show you."

Emma and I followed Mr. Henriques out the front door and onto the wraparound lanai. He led us around to the back. From the corner of the lanai, we could see the rental unit through the leggy papala and bushy strawberry guava that I kept at roof-height for privacy's sake. On the far side of the rental unit was Mr. Henriques's house. It was a little shabby, and the metal roof needed repainting. But he kept his lawn neatly-trimmed and his carport well-organized, and he never let mail or newspapers stack up.

"I don't hear anything," I said. "Really, they were making enough noise to disturb you inside your house?"

"Well it's quiet now," he admitted.

"What did you hear before?" Emma asked.

"They was arguing," he said. "Like, real loud kine."

"Mr. Henriques, if you think there's an actual emergency—"

"I know. Call 9-1-1 right away," he said sheepishly. "Otherwise give 'em their privacy."

"It's wonderful to hear your concern for your neighbors' well-being, truly," I said.

"Well, I got no one else to look after these days. Might as well make myself useful, ah?"

Instead of using the conversational pause to take his leave, Henriques leaned on the railing of the lanai as if he were settling in for a long chat.

"Eh, Mrs. Gonsalves, your husband here?"

Emma started to answer but I cut her off.

"Donnie's out at the moment." If Mr. Henriques knew that Donnie and baby Francesca were traveling on the mainland and that I was here alone, he would only ramp up his helpful visits.

"I was wondering how come Donnie's Drive-Inn was all closed up," he said. "You're not closing for good, ah?"

"No, not at all. It's just for a couple of weeks."

"You and Mr. Gonsalves getting divorced? That's gonna be hard for you, single working mom with a new baby."

"No! Of course not. We're just doing some renovations. We thought this would be a perfect time. The college and high school spring break both happened to fall on the same dates this year, so half of Mahina's vacationing in Vegas right now."

Including my husband and daughter. Donnie thought it was important for Francesca to meet his family members. His uncle in Las Vegas, for one, wasn't getting any younger. My appalling stepson Davison lived there too, and had a kid of his own, about Francesca's age.

Mr. Henriques frowned.

"You think I should talk to Mr. Ladd? You know, give him some hints about how to treat the wife? It's not right for them to be shouting at each other like that."

"I don't think Molly's gonna let you," Emma said.

"Look," I said, "It's true, I am being protective of Jandie and her husband. When they signed their lease, they specifically said they wanted to live somewhere quiet, where fans wouldn't bother them. At first I thought they were being a little extreme, but now? I'm starting to understand. I mean, just today I had someone I thought was my best friend, pretend to come by to visit me, but all along it was a ruse to wangle a face-to-face with Jandie."

"Hey!" Emma objected.

"And then a former coworker who I haven't seen in years pops up and demands I arm-twist Jandie into featuring this woman's horrible little dogs on her social media. The whole reason Jandie and her husband are in Mahina in the first place is because they want a break from the spotlight."

"Oh yeah, Jandie, maybe," Mr. Henriques said. "But I think Mr. Ladd would like to have a little bit of that spotlight shining on him again."

CHAPTER FOUR

By the time Mr. Henriques finally left, it was close to lunchtime. Emma wandered into the kitchen and opened the freezer side of the refrigerator.

"Wow, Donnie set you up good. There's like a year's worth of food in here. What a *mensch*."

"I know. It was thoughtful of him. It's strange not having Donnie and the baby here. The house seems so empty. I think I'm starting to miss them."

I heard the microwave run. Emma wandered back out to the living room holding a bowl piled high with steaming chow fun and pulled a chair up next to where I was working.

"What are you doing, Molly?"

I lifted my hands from the keyboard.

"What do you mean, what am I doing? I do all kinds of stuff on the computer."

"Yeah, but you're doing it secretively. I can tell cause the sneaky way you're typing."

Emma stared at me accusingly as she chewed her chow fun.

"Fine. I was searching for Edward Ladd. My tenant. It's a common name, unfortunately."

Emma pointed at me dramatically.

"Aha! Stalking your tenants. After you told everyone else to leave 'em alone."

"Yeah, well, the difference is, what I'm doing doesn't bother them because they don't know I'm doing it."

Emma scooted her chair closer and peered at my computer screen.

"What are you looking for? You find anything good?"

"Not yet. I was wondering what Mr. Henriques meant about Ladd missing the spotlight. Should I know who he is? Is he some infamous serial killer or something?"

"Why don't you just ask him?"

"What, ask my tenant if he's a serial killer?"

"No, ask Mr. Henriques what he meant. He's lonely, Molly, can't you tell? He'd love for someone to listen to all his conspiracy theories an' stuff."

"I'd really rather not."

Emma shoved my shoulder.

"Eh, Molly. Try Ed Ladd. Instead of Edward."

"I already did."

"How about Teddy or Ted?"

"Oh, good idea. Hm. No, nope, no. Oh my goodness, that is *definitely* not him."

"Put safe search on," Emma suggested.

"Oh yeah, good idea. Okay, let's try again. I'm still not… wait a second. What? No way. Seriously?"

Emma bounced impatiently in her chair.

"What is it, Molly?"

"Hang on, let me show you something."

I went to my bookshelf and pulled down a book. I was unpleasantly surprised to see it was speckled with brownish-orange mold. The pages looked chewed around the edges.

"What's that?" Emma asked.

"I guess I haven't read this in a while. Mahina weather isn't great for books, is it?"

Emma took the book from me.

"Ew. You should buy a dehumidifier. Where'd you get this?"

"I bought it for myself as a treat after I left my corporate job."

"Seriously, Molly? You used to have a real job? How come I never knew this?"

"It didn't last long. It's not something I care to discuss."

"Huh." Emma leafed through the pages. "I thought about going into industry, you know. Lotta my old classmates ended up there. Working at seed companies, or chemical companies. It's good money. How'd you like it?"

"I didn't," I said. "Everything was about bringing in money and tying yourself in knots catering to entitled, unreasonable clients."

"Oh yes, so very different from teaching at Mahina State."

"I am aware of the irony."

"You should toss this and get a new copy." Emma handed the book back to me. "It's falling apart."

"No, I'm keeping it," I said. "It's out of print. And it's signed by the author. Maybe it'll be worth something someday."

"The author? Who you think is living in your rental unit right now?"

"It could be him. What do you think?"

Emma turned the book over and scowled at the author photo on the back cover.

"This guy has hair."

"Well, it's been a couple of decades."

"Eh Molly, you know who would be interested in this? Pat."

"Emma, that's a great idea! Pat can get to the bottom of this."

Pat Flanagan used to work the crime beat for our local paper, the *County Courier*, before they laid off most of their staff. He started his own newsblog, *Island Confidential*, and took a job teaching composition at Mahina State, which is how Emma and I met him. The three of us were inseparable, until he moved to Honolulu to take a job at an acclaimed alternative weekly. The move was great for Pat's career, a completely rational decision on his part. But I still missed him. I'm pretty sure Emma did too.

"Should I call him right now?" I asked.

"Good idea. I'll get us some wine."

"I guess it is after noon. But not Donnie's good wine, Emma. It costs a fortune, and I would never say it to him, but I honestly can't tell the difference. Can you go into the pantry and grab a box? Try not to knock over the wall of Spam."

CHAPTER FIVE

BY THAT EVENING IT WAS RAINING SO HARD IT WOULD HAVE
been dangerous for Emma to drive home, even if she had
been sober. I set her up on the living room couch with a
blanket and pillow. She was out by nine. It took me a little
longer to get to sleep. People describe the sound of rain falling
on a metal roof as "restful." Which, sure, if you like the sound
of someone pouring buckshot into a metal garbage can right
over your head.

The next morning I thought at first I had gotten up early.
But I hadn't. It just seemed dark because of the dense cloud
cover.

I walked out to the kitchen and brewed myself a cup of
coffee. Emma was fast asleep on the couch, unbothered by the
rumbling of the coffee maker. I took my cup out to the lanai
and watched sheets of rain sweep across the cemetery behind
my house.

I saw something move out on the lawn. A big red-and-
white golf umbrella propelled by a scurrying little pair of legs.
My neighbor Mr. Henriques was heading my way.

I ran around to the front door and headed him off before
he could knock and wake up everyone in the house. But then I

remembered Donnie and the baby were on the mainland and the only person inside was Emma.

Mr. Henriques shook out his umbrella, spattering both of us. He apologized and set it down on the porch. I invited him inside and tried to jostle Emma awake, but she muttered something and pulled a pillow over her head.

"Would you like a cup of coffee, Mr. Henriques?" I asked.

"Do you have orange juice?"

"No, I'm afraid I still don't."

"Coffee's okay then."

I brewed him a cup, and a second cup for me, and set out the cream and sugar on the dining table.

"Sorry to bother you again," he said as he got seated. "Thanks for the coffee, ah? I thought I should tell you right away."

Mr. Henriques dumped the entire contents of the cream carton into his coffee cup, leaving me to drink mine black.

"So, Mr. Henriques, what is it you have to tell me? It must be important to come out in this weather." I sipped and tried not to wrinkle my nose. Mizuno Mart house brand coffee without any cream in it tastes like paving tar.

"There's no one in the house," said Mr. Henriques.

"I don't understand. You and I are sitting right here, and Emma is over there on the couch. Wait. You don't mean…"

"Mr. Henriques looked embarrassed.

"My *renters'* house? Were you spying on Jandie and her husband?"

"Nah, nah, not spying. I saw the jalousies was open. The rainwater was going to get in an' cause damage."

"Oh. Well that seems reasonable, I guess."

"I went over an' knocked and no one answered. I wanted to make sure everything was ok. I know you said stay away from 'em, only I suspected something was wrong. I was worried about their safety."

"Do I smell coffee?" I heard Emma ask from the couch. "Eh, howzit, Mr. Henriques."

"Mr. Henriques was just telling me he saw the windows open on the rental unit," I said. "And when he knocked, no one answered."

"I'm listening. I'm gonna make myself some coffee." Emma ambled into the kitchen.

"So what happened then?" I asked.

"Well I went inside to see what was going on."

"Okay. I think that's technically breaking and entering. So what did you find? A dead body or something?"

"No." He fidgeted. "Nobody there, the house was empty. They was gone."

"Gone like empty? Like they'd packed up and left?"

"No, the furniture and everything was there."

"So you broke into the rental unit when the occupants were away."

Mr. Henriques concentrated very hard on sipping his creamy coffee.

"I'm glad you're being honest with me, Mr. Henriques, but do you understand why it was a bad idea to go inside? What if someone had been inside and thought you were a burglar? You could've gotten shot."

Emma brought her coffee over and sat down at the table with us. She picked up the cream carton, shook it, and put it back down. She sighed and spooned four heaping spoonsful of sugar into her cup.

"You see any broken windows?" Emma asked. "Blood spatters anywhere?"

"No," I said before he could answer. "They just happened to be out. Let's hope they don't notice and please, Mr. Henriques, never go into their house unless they specifically invite you."

"But where'd they go? They shouldn't be out in this weather," he objected.

"*You* were out in this weather," I said testily. "You walked over here."

"But they left the windows open," he said.

"Good for you, Mr. Henriques," Emma said. "You stopped the rain from coming in and now Molly and Donnie don't have to pay to fix water damage."

"I appreciate your good intentions," I said. "Next time you see something amiss, please just knock. If they don't answer, come here and let Donnie or me know. We'll figure out what to do."

"A lot of people have guns, you know," Emma said. "You coulda been shot."

"I already told him that, Emma."

His eyes widened.

"Do you think Jandie would shoot me?"

"Nah, I can't see Jandie shooting anyone," Emma said. "But the husband might, you know."

"Eh, when I was inside, I saw they got da kine, a big saltwater aquarium."

"They what?" I said.

"I got one aquarium too, you know," Mr. Henriques said. "Small kine. Eh, I just caught a couple snowflake eel down at the tidepools. Maybe I could give 'em one."

"Did you see any water damage?" I asked.

Emma reached over and shoved my shoulder. "Who cares about water damage, Molly? You get *Jandie Brand* staying at your house."

"Yes I do. Jandie Brand and her saltwater aquarium."

I watched Mr. Henriques tip his cup back to finish the last drop of his cream-with-coffee.

"Thank you so much for this, Mrs. Gonsalves." He wiped his mouth with the back of his hand.

"No problem," I said. "Always a pleasure."

"Cream in my coffee is a real treat for me."

"I know. I like it too."

"I don't get to enjoy it much. I'm on a fixed income, you know."

"Oh." Well, *that* made me feel bad. "Um, look, Mr. Henriques, when we closed down the Drive-Inn to do the renovations? We had to bring home a lot of food. More than we could possibly eat. Could I get you to take home a tray or two? It's frozen, so it'll last."

"Oh, I don't know, Mrs. Gonsalves…"

"Please. It's just taking up room in the freezer. You'd be doing me a favor."

Emma and I stood on the porch and watched Mr. Henriques make his way back to his house. In one hand he held his giant golf umbrella. In the other he clutched a Mizuno Mart shopping tote containing foil trays of chow mein and chicken katsu. One protein and one vegetable.

"It *is* kind of weird for Jandie and her husband to be out when the weather's like this," Emma said.

"Maybe they were spending time with friends, and they got stuck and had to stay overnight. Just like you did," I said.

"Sure," Emma said. "Maybe."

CHAPTER SIX

By the time Emma and I had gotten the dishes washed up, the rain had diminished from "deluge" to "normal for Mahina." I did my express-dress (quick shower, minimal makeup, glop on some hair product and hope for the best) and made the short drive to morning Mass at St. Damien's. My showing up baby-less did not go unnoticed. A pack of aunties intercepted me on the way back to my car and would not let me leave until I had assured them that Francesca was fine, Donnie was perfectly capable of providing her safe passage to the Mainland and back, and the closure of Donnie's Drive-Inn was only temporary. We'd soon be back in business better than ever, I insisted. It was more social interaction than I'd bargained for, and I sped home with the sole objective of collapsing into bed.

By the time I pulled up to my house, the rain had ceased, leaving the street steaming in the sun. Mr. Ladd—Tedd Ladd, as I now knew him to be—was in his carport, hosing off the tires of his truck.

I parked in the garage and walked down to the rental unit to say hello. He'd seen me pull in, so it would seem antisocial if I just ignored him and went inside. I was also curious about two things: Was he in fact the formerly-famous cartoonist who had signed my book decades earlier? And did he have any idea Mr. Henriques had been snooping around inside their house?

"Looks like we have a new water feature," he remarked. I followed his gaze to the graveyard that backed up to the edge of our properties. A vast, shimmering lake (or so it seemed) was studded with the tops of gravestones.

"I happened to notice your car wasn't in the carport earlier today," I said. "I was a little worried. Because of the flash flood warning. They say to avoid driving long distances. You know, turn around, don't drown."

"*You* just drove somewhere," he retorted.

"Yes. I went to Mass this morning. St. Damien's is less than half a mile away. I actually could've walked."

"Mass, huh? Whatever gets you through, I guess. Anyway, looks like we're all safe and sound. So nothing to worry about."

"OK, great. Well, have a nice Sunday." I turned to go back to my house.

"Jandie wasn't feeling well," he said.

I turned back around.

"We went to look for a drugstore. You know. Female stuff." Ladd gestured vaguely at the front of his cargo shorts.

"Well, next time, if she needs some ibuprofen or a heating pad or something, she can come over and borrow it," I said.

"It's no big deal," Ladd started winding up the hose. "She'll be fine."

"Good. I'm glad. Okay, you both have a great day."

"How'd it go?" Emma said when I walked in. "I saw you talking to the husband. Does he know Mr. Henriques went into his house?"

"I wish he really had stolen his stupid fish," I said.

"Who stole whose fish, what?"

"Nothing."

"Eh, your hedge in the back is looking kinda raggedy, yeah?" Emma said. "Is Kaycee still doing your yardwork?"

I went over to the window and saw that the back hedge could in fact be described as raggedy.

"She's supposed to come by today," I said. "In fact she's supposed to be here now. I don't know what's going on. She normally does good work."

Kaycee Kabua was a Mahina State agriculture graduate who had started her own landscaping business. She had been doing Emma and Yoshi's yard and Emma had recommended her to me. It seemed to me Kaycee's work had been slipping lately, but I didn't want to say anything that would make Emma think I didn't appreciate the referral. Besides, if Kaycee was having any personal issues, I didn't want to make things worse for her by talking her down to Emma.

CHAPTER SEVEN

WHEN KAYCEE STILL HADN'T MADE AN APPEARANCE IN MY backyard an hour later, I moved from annoyance to worry and decided to call her. But when I went out to the back lanai where the reception is better, I spotted her on the other end of the yard, behind the rental unit. Fair enough, she was supposed to be looking after both properties. Although it struck me that since the new tenants had moved in, she seemed to spend a lot more time on their side of the lot.

When she saw me walking toward her, she put down the long-handled implement she had been poking into the trees.

"Eh professor," she said.

"Aren't you hot?" I asked. She was wearing a hoodie, with the hood fastened so tightly that only her eyes and nose were visible. Kaycee was in her twenties but still cute in the way that babies are cute, with plump cheeks and round, dark eyes.

Kaycee shrugged.

"The little fire ants like drop down the back of your neck, that's why."

"Oh. Is it better to come by when it's cooler?"

"Nah, I'm fine."

"Okay. Well. Do you think you'll be able to get to the other part of the hedge today?"

A single hedge ran along the back of the property, separating the backyards of 25 Uakoko Street (where Donnie and I lived) and 25b (the rental unit) from the cemetery beyond. The hedge behind the rental unit was neatly-trimmed and free of weeds. Our side, by contrast, looked like it had gone on a three-day bender.

I shouldn't have been surprised. Kaycee was a Jandista (a fan of Jandie Brand) so I could understand why she'd linger close to Jandie's house, trimming leaves while hoping to catch a glimpse of her idol.

"Sure, I'll get to it today. Eh," She cleared her throat and looked around. "the wife went missing or what?"

"Not that I know of. But if you see anything out of place, please let me know."

"Okay Professor, will do. Eh, no worries, I'm gonna get to the other side today, even 'em up, make 'em look nice, yeah?"

When I got inside, Emma was sitting at the dining table with her laptop open, drinking wine out of a mug and reading the news.

"More rain coming," she said. "That's not gonna be good. Not gonna be able to paddle for a while."

"Why not?"

"A bunch of cesspools are gonna overflow and it's all gonna run into the ocean. All the farm runoff too."

"Thank you for reminding me why I never go into the ocean."

"We'll get you out there one of these days."

"Nope."

"Oh, I emailed Pat about da kine. Cartoon guy."

"Heard back?" I asked.

"Not yet. I gotta finish up this report, and get some grading done, and then I'm done for the day. I know, I'm a heathen for working on Sunday."

I tidied up the kitchen and then folded laundry until Emma was done. Laundry doesn't count as work in my mind, because I don't get paid to do it.

"Finally." Emma closed her laptop and pushed up from the couch. "Time for happy hour."

"What was taking so long?" I opened a new bottle of wine (my cheap and cheerful red blend, not Donnie's fancy Sangiovese) and filled two repurposed furikake jars.

"Stupid online class. Right on," Emma said as she took a small jar. "You got the Mahina stemware."

"Yeah, I don't see the point of an actual stem on your glass," I said. "It just makes it more prone to tip over."

"Want to go outside?" Emma said. "I've been indoors all day."

"Okay. Let me check and make sure Kaycee's finished up."

"Why?"

"I told her to work on the whole hedge and not just the part near the rental unit. I don't want her to think I'm checking up on her or don't trust her to do her job properly."

"You don't trust anyone to do their job properly," Emma said.

The hedge was evenly trimmed, giving Emma and me a clear view into the cemetery from the back lanai. The twilight had an unusual reddish tinge to it. The air hung close and heavy. I felt mosquitos lurking nearby, sniffing for a gap in the repellent I'd doused myself in.

"Your hedge looks good," Emma said. "Kaycee does good work, yeah?"

"Once you can get her to stop lingering around hoping to catch a glimpse of her idol."

"Give her a break, Molly. It's not like we get a lot of celebrities in Mahina."

"Conform in Speech, and Dress and Thought," I said, "And you'll Be Promoted When You Ought."

"What is that from?" Emma asked.

"Safety Worm. Tedd Ladd's cartoon character," I said. "Safety Worm is like an amoral Jiminy Cricket for careerist office workers. There's a second line. Speak the Truth and Have Your Say, and You'll Get Two Weeks' Severance Pay. Wow, I hadn't thought of that in years. But it came right back. It's been lurking in my subconscious this whole time."

"Catchy," Emma said. "You should put that in your email signature. It would be perfect for you College of Commerce guys."

"Do people even get severance pay anymore?"

"You okay?" Emma asked.

"Mr. Henriques and Kaycee have both noticed Jandie's gone," I said. "It's not just me."

"How did the husband seem when you talked to him?" Emma asked. "Did he seem nervous or like he had a guilty conscience?"

"Not at all. He seemed smug and dismissive."

"He goes out in the middle of a storm, comes home by himself, hoses off the car, no trace of the wife," Emma said.

"He claimed she was inside," I said. "Or implied it, anyway."

"Uh huh. Do you believe him?" Emma asked.

"Emma, I don't want to get sucked into some *Rear Window*-type voyeuristic obsession with my renters."

"In *Rear Window*, there was an actual murder," Emma reminded me.

"He said she wasn't feeling well. She has 'female trouble' apparently."

"Couldn't ask for a better opening," Emma said. "We're female."

"It's already dark. I don't want to do anything dumb after dark."

"Tomorrow then," Emma said.

"Fine."

CHAPTER EIGHT

THE NEXT MORNING, EMMA AND I WERE IN THE KITCHEN, packing up a "Feel better" package for Jandie Brand. Or rather, I packed while Emma noodged me. She would say "supervised."

"Okay, we've got ibuprofen, caffeine pills, eyeshades, and a bottle of wine" I said. "I don't know about the heating pad, though."

"What's wrong with the heating pad?"

"Something chewed through the cord. Ew, what's living in my closet and chewing through things?"

"Look, there's mold on it," Emma added.

I dropped the heating pad into the garbage can.

"Lemme call the house." Emma dialed the phone.

"If we're just doing all this to call Ladd's bluff, Emma, I don't know that we need—"

Emma waved her arm to shush me.

"No, I wanna go home, and make sure my doofus husband and my idiot brother haven't burned the house down. Oh, hey, Jonah. Howzit. Yeah, good. Good. She's fine. Listen, I'm gonna come by real quick an' grab the heating pad. It's...you did what?"

Emma leaned her elbows on the kitchen counter and planted her free hand on her face.

"No, Jonah, it's not. It's a *terrible* idea. Lucky you never get electrocuted...oh yeah? Well you deserved it. I'll just use the hot water bottle. Yeah, the red one...what do you mean it doesn't work? Never mind, I'll be right over. Don't go anywhere. In fact, don't do anything. That's right, I do mean stand still and hold your breath till I get there."

I barely had time to finish a cup of coffee before Emma was back.

"You must've been lucky with traffic." I took the hot water bottle from her and placed it into the gift bag "This looks fine. What's wrong with it?"

"Nothing's wrong with it. My idiot brother didn't realize that even though it's called a hot water bottle, you still gotta heat the water up yourself before you put it in. Ready to go?"

"Ready as I'll ever be."

Emma and I squelched across the wet lawn to the rental unit. The rain had cleared but the ground was saturated and soggy.

"Emma, do you think Jandie's really sick?"

"You think her husband's lying."

"No. Yes. Maybe. Fifty-fifty. I don't know. OK, look. If he's telling the truth, then we're being good neighbors."

"And if he's not, we're on our way to visit a murderous psychopath who just killed his wife."

I stopped.

"Should we go back?"

"Nah. He probably already saw us out the window anyway. Come on."

"There are so many places to hide a body around here," I said. "Lava tubes, rivers, a whole ocean—"

"There's a whole freakin' cemetery right next door, don't forget," Emma said.

The door of the rental unit opened as we approached it. Tedd Ladd was unshaven and looked gaunt.

"Eh, good morning," Emma said. "We brought over some things for your wife."

"For Jandie? Why?"

"You mentioned she wasn't feeling well," I said.

"Lady troubles." Emma elbowed me, which reminded me I was holding the gift bag.

Ladd held the door open just wide enough to reach out through the crack.

"I'll make sure she gets it."

"Maybe we can come in and help her set up the hot water bottle," Emma said. "They're tricky for some people."

"No thanks. We're fine." Ladd tried to push the door shut, but couldn't. Emma had placed her foot over the door stop, and she was wearing hiking boots. She'd planned ahead for this, apparently.

"Why don't you want us to come in?" Emma challenged him.

"Emma," I said, "we can just go…"

Ladd stepped back and Emma and I fairly tumbled into the living room.

"She's not here." Ladd crossed his arms and looked at the floor. "I didn't want to tell you. The truth is, I don't know where she is. You might as well come in."

We stepped inside and he closed the door behind us, which made me a little nervous. Right away I saw the aquarium Mr. Henriques had been talking about. It was huge, occupying the entire length of the counter that separated the living-dining area from the kitchen. The emergency generator had been moved inside from the carport and sat underneath the counter, apparently ready to rescue the aquarium if the power went out.

I walked over for a closer look.

"Lovely aquarium." I know little to nothing about

aquariums. I wanted to check for water damage on the countertop without being obvious about it. The aquarium *was* lovely, in the usual way aquariums are. It contained waving greenery, a swarm of tiny electric-blue fish, a clump of fleshy anemones, and a couple of those things that look like flat lemons swimming around. Sitting on the bottom was a brown lump with a ridge of lacy spines and a grouchy expression. The countertop seemed free of water damage. So far.

"I can watch it for hours," Ladd said. "I think my next addition will be a snowflake eel. My sources tell me you can find them in the tidepools in Pohaku."

I knew which tidepools he was talking about. They were right outside the Maritime Club. Emma was a club member. I don't know whether Ladd knew this, or whether he was angling (ha!) for an invitation from her, but Emma didn't say anything.

"So what's going on with Jandie?" I asked. I thought that would be his cue to invite us to sit down, but he didn't. Instead the three of us stood and stared at the aquarium. It looked like something that belonged in a hotel lobby, I thought. It was completely out of place in a little rental house. Still, I found myself staring at it.

"She went out, and she hasn't come back," Ladd said. "I don't know anyone here, so I didn't…Jandie's a free spirit, and I don't want to seem overbearing. She would hate it if I called the police just because she happened to be out of cell phone range."

"There's a lot of places on the island that are out of range," Emma took out her phone. "You been checking her posts?"

Ladd rubbed the back of his neck.

"Of course I have. I mean, not in the last five minutes."

"This one's timestamped this morning. Mahina rainbow." Emma held out her phone for Ladd to see.

Ladd took the phone from her, shook his head, and handed it back.

"That's a pre-scheduled post. She took it a while ago."

"Is it usual for her to go out on a photoshoot overnight?" I asked.

He shrugged.

"She's never done it before without letting me know first. Is there anything dangerous she might not know about?"

Emma strolled over to the living room couch and plunked down on the couch. I followed her over, and Ed Ladd followed me.

"Mr. Ladd. Edward. May I call you Edward?" Emma said.

"Ed's fine."

"Ed, this is a beautiful island, which is probably why you came in the first place. But what a lotta newcomers don't realize is there's a million ways to die here."

"Emma," I said, "I don't know whether—"

"Molly," Emma interrupted me, "he asked if there's anything dangerous here. An' it's good he asked, cause lots of tourists don't ask the right questions."

"I wouldn't call us *tourists* necessarily—" Ladd said.

"They assume the whole island chain was designed by Disneyland safety engineers or something," Emma went on. "Until someone gets swept out to the ocean, or drops into a lava tube, or falls off a cliff while they're hiking—"

"Emma!" I shook my head.

Ladd held up his hand.

"No, I asked. I need to know."

"Hey, at least no get poisonous snakes," Emma reassured him.

"I believe you mean venomous, not poisonous," Ladd said. "A poisonous snake can only hurt you if you try to eat it. But I take your point."

Emma's lip twitched dangerously. She does not like being corrected.

"Well we should go." I went over to Emma and pulled her up from the couch by the elbow. "So try the fire department first, they're good with rescuing hikers. Or just call 9-1-1 and let the dispatcher decide. Better Jandie gets mad at you for being concerned than have her stuck at the bottom of a ravine with a broken leg and no one to help her. Okay, bye, let me know if you need anything."

"What's the rush?" Emma shook me off and straightened out her t-shirt as we walked back toward the house.

"You were going to do something bad to him."

"Molly, *I* know the difference between poisonous and venomous. I said poisonous for *his* benefit."

"I know."

"It's like if I knock on your door, and you say who is it, I don't say it is I. I say it's me. It's casual conversation, I'm not in front of a classroom. It's da kine, what's that thing you English majors call it?"

"Maybe he was trying to be helpful. He doesn't know you're a biology professor."

"*Putz*. Him, not you. Know what? I think he killed Jandie."

"You think he murdered his wife? Because he corrected you?"

"Because he's a freakin' psychopath. And I know that's not a real thing and it's actually called antisocial personality disorder so don't correct me."

"I wouldn't dream of it. Emma, you go on inside. I'm going to pick up the mail. I know I shouldn't say this, because they prepaid a six-month lease. But I don't really like him either."

CHAPTER NINE

ON THE WAY TO THE MAILBOX I NOTICED A FOLDED PIECE OF lime-green paper tucked under one of the windshield wipers on Emma's car. I plucked it out and brought it inside.

Emma was already set up at the kitchen counter with a box of wine and two full glasses.

"Eh, no look at me all judgmental li'dat Molly. It's...hang on a second."

She pulled out her phone and frowned at the screen.

"Fifty-seven, fifty-eight, fifty nine, okay, *now* it's after noon."

"You got mail." I handed her the folded flyer. It turned out to be a "friendly" warning from the Uakoko Street Homeowner's Association. Emma gulped her wine and plunked the glass down aggressively on the paper, right over the clip art of the smiling sun.

"Since when am I not allowed to park on the grass?" she demanded. "What, I'm supposed to park on your narrow little street and block traffic?"

"I guess so, because apparently if you don't, I have to pay a fine. Dangit. When did they become so zealous? Honestly, I didn't even know we had a homeowner's association. I mean, not an active one. This is the first time I've ever seen anything from them besides the postcard in the mail reminding me to pay the annual fee."

"Maybe it's cause you get Jandie living here."

"Well joke's on them, because Jandie's missing. Seriously, you think they've gone all activist about keeping cars off the lawns just because we have a minor celebrity living here?"

"Not just a celebrity, Molly. An influencer. Her whole *shtick* is taking pictures and sharing them with the entire world. Maybe your association thinks a car on your lawn's bad for the neighborhood image."

"Image? Uakoko Street? I mean, I like living here, but I think I'd describe it as 'unpretentious' at best."

"You got a better explanation?"

"I guess not. Hey, since it is actually lunchtime, you want something to eat?"

"Are you cooking?" Emma asked suspiciously.

"No. Donnie left us a bunch of frozen food from the Drive-Inn."

"Oh, yeah that sounds perfect. Eh, I forget to tell you Pat's on his way over."

"Pat Flanagan? Is on his way here?"

"Yeah. I texted him about da kine, Ladd. Turns out his editor thinks an article about a washed-up cartoonist living in the backwoods of Mahina sounds interesting. Go figure."

I checked the oven to make sure it was empty (an old habit from before I was married, when I used the oven as shoe storage overflow). I set it to heat and selected a tinfoil pan from the freezer. Chicken katsu and teriyaki beef, according to the masking-tape label.

"Do you want to invite Yoshi and Jonah to join us?" I asked Emma.

"Nah. Yoshi's got a thing with his paddling club and Jonah's going with him. I can set the table."

Emma got up and started clearing away the glasses and the empty bottle.

"Oh, thanks for clearing that off."

"Yeah, I don't need Pat getting all judgey about us day drinking."

"Yoshi and your brother aren't going paddling in this weather, are they?"

"Nah, they're going down there to move the canoes away from the bayfront. In case there's a storm surge. Afterwards they're all gonna go back to the house and party."

"Sounds festive."

"Yeah, after a couple drinks the ukuleles come out and then the singing starts."

"It sounds nice," I said.

"Sure, it is. For the first seven or eight hours."

"Do you want to stay here tonight?" I asked.

"Oh yeah, that's a good idea. We can catch up with Pat and not worry about driving home in the bad weather."

"I'd offer you a spare toothbrush but I'm guessing when you went home this morning you brought back a packed overnight bag."

"You know me so well. Seriously, though, I owe you. If there's one sound that's worse than Yoshi snoring, it's him trying to sing 'Hawaiian Superman' after a few beers."

Pat showed up at my door about half an hour later. His head was still shaved but he'd grown a goatee, which I was surprised to see was graying. I'd always thought of Pat as young.

"I forgot how much I hate riding in the Sampan," was the first thing he said as he walked in. I watched the open-air wagon waddle back down the street.

"I like the Sampan," I said as I closed the door. "It's old-timey, and it's very Mahina."

"Pat hates it cause his legs are too long." Emma came out of the kitchen. "Eh, Pat, good to see you."

43

Pat hugged Emma, then me. His leather jacket smelled wet and cold.

"Sure it's okay if I stay over?" he asked. "Donnie doesn't mind?"

"I'm sure he wouldn't. Go put your stuff in the guest room, come back and we'll have lunch. I hope you're hungry."

When he'd gone into the guest room I remembered Emma was spending the night too.

"Sorry, Emma, you can have the nursery. I'll bring an air mattress in."

"No worries. I like the couch. Eh, Pat looks good, yeah, with the beard?"

"He looks distinguished," I said. "Unsettlingly so. Huh. I wonder whether he's seeing someone."

"I'm right here," Pat said as he seated himself at the table.

"That was fast," I said. "So are you seeing someone?"

"A gentleman doesn't kiss and tell. Hey, they did a good job, whoever built your rental unit. The style matches your house."

"Konishi Construction," I said. "They're the only game in town, so good thing they know what they're doing."

I pulled the pan out of the oven and carefully positioned it on the three potholders Emma had placed on the table. I'd asked her to set out four, one for each corner of the pan, but she'd insisted three was more stable, like a camera tripod.

"Oh, the food looks great," Pat said. "All I've had to eat today is an overpriced airport muffin."

"Thanks," I said. "Reheated katsu and teriyaki beef served in its original foil pan, just as nature intended. Nothing but the best for my guests."

"It's from Donnie's Drive-Inn," Emma assured him.

"Oh right, in case you were afraid it was something I'd made."

"So how's it going with your celebrity tenants?" Pat asked.

"The wife's missing," I said.

"Jandie Brand," Emma added.

Pat set the serving tongs down and straightened up from his customary slouch.

"Missing? Officially?"

"They went out for a drive, and only the husband came back," Emma said. "And then we went over this morning and he admitted she was missing."

"In the middle of a hurricane and a flash flood warning," I added.

"Is anyone gonna look for her?" Pat asked.

"The husband said he was gonna get help," Emma said. "I'm not sure I believe him."

"So you think he's *the* Tedd Ladd, huh?" Pat downed his coffee went to the kitchen to brew himself another.

"Maybe?" I said. "It's hard to tell. Edward Ladd is a common name. And it has to be ten years since he was actually famous. Pat, how can you drink coffee all day? Doesn't it keep you up?"

Pat came back and set down his coffee.

"Come on, doesn't that smell great? *Ten* years ago? Try twenty. That's when Tedd Ladd was in his heyday."

"Twenty years? Are you sure? Wow, we're old."

"Yeah, I can't see it being the same guy," Emma said. "Jandie's husband just seems like some middle-aged loser who likes to stare at his fish tank."

"It's a pretty spectacular fish tank," I said. "It takes up the entire kitchen counter."

"Worried about water damage in your new rental unit?" Pat asked.

"Why would you assume that would be my main concern?"

"It tracks though," Pat said. "Ever notice how many celebrities get sick of dealing with people and decide they'd rather be around animals instead?"

45

"I don't think I ever heard of this guy Ladd before," Emma said.

"He might not have been that popular in Hawaii," Pat said. "You think he's involved in his wife's disappearance? It's usually the spouse."

"Yes," Emma said.

"No," I said.

"He's a has-been and can't stand his wife's success," Emma said.

"Emma doesn't like him. Emma, I thought you just said you didn't think he was the famous Tedd Ladd. How can he be a has-been?"

"Who cares?" Emma retorted. "He's old enough to be her dad. And he looks like a jerky stick with glasses."

The roar of a motorcycle stopped abruptly outside my front door.

"Now, old boy!" somebody was saying in a plummy voice. "Steady, old chap! I've got something for you."

CHAPTER TEN

I LOOKED OUT THE FRONT WINDOW AND SAW OUR BUSINESS LAW instructor, Harriet Holmes, dismounting her 1966 Triumph Bonneville. She bent down to reach something on the ground. I realized she was feeding something to one of the neighborhood's feral cats.

"Why is Harriet here?" I said. "And how does she know where I live?"

"Harriet Holmes?" Pat asked. "Wow, I showed up at the right time."

Pat Flanagan had never met Harriet Holmes, but he knew very well who she was.

Harriet Holmes's arrival in Mahina had coincided with certain events newsworthy enough to make the national media outlets. Harriet currently taught law and ethics in the College of Commerce. Recently retired from Oxford, she thought teaching in "the tropics" (Mahina) would be a "jolly wheeze." As chair of the management department, I was technically her supervisor, to the extent anyone could "supervise" Harriet Holmes.

She bounded up the steps and hammered on the door. As I opened up she barged inside.

On first impression, Harriet Holmes is not glamorous. She is in late middle age and squarely built, with chopped mouse-gray hair that perpetually looks like it's been squashed under a hat. (Because it has.) Harriet eschews cosmetics, reeks of pipe tobacco, and dresses like she's on her way to muck out the stables. Men find Harriet irresistible.

"Ah, what ho, Barda, Nakamura." Harriet removed her flat cap and stuffed it in one of the pockets of her field coat. "Hullo, who's this fair Fenian?"

Pat sprang up from the dining table so fast he practically knocked his chair over.

"I'm Pat Flanagan. It's great to meet you."

"Tea?" I offered. Harriet cheerfully (if unflatteringly) replied, "I'll make it."

I helped Harriet locate the kettle and our rarely-used supply of loose tea. Having exhausted my usefulness in the matter, I left her to it. Pat, Emma, and I seated ourselves at the counter so we could converse while Harriet worked her tea magic in my kitchen.

"Harriet, this is such a nice surprise," I said. "What brings you by?"

"Nigel and I are looking to let a cottage," she said, "We've found something just up the street. Would be jolly fun to be neighbors, eh, Barda? We can ride to work together. Save you a bit on petrol."

"Now *there's* an idea." That I planned never to follow up on. I imagined myself riding on the back of Harriet's skinny-wheeled Triumph, splashing through muddy potholes while hanging on for dear life.

"What's wrong with the place you got now?" Emma asked. "You're right on the Hanakoa River. How come you wanna move?"

"The river's beastly at the moment. It's all muddy water and debris churning past, not pleasant to look at in the least. Nigel says he feels he's about to tip straight into it every time he steps out onto the lanai. Oh, and he doesn't get on with Clyde."

Emma reached under the counter and nudged Pat's knee.

"Clyde Hamamoto." Emma whispered. "Harriet's good friend from the motorcycle club. He's their *landlord*."

Pat nodded knowingly.

"Uakoko Street suits us both down to the ground," Harriet was saying. "Nigel's taking ages to finish his manuscript. He needs to be somewhere quiet where he can write without the rushing water breaking his concentration."

"What's Nigel writing?" Pat asked.

"His prison memoir," Harriet replied proudly. "The location's perfect. One couldn't hope for quieter neighbors than yours."

I was confused for a minute, as I didn't think the residents of Uakoko Street were particularly noiseless.

"She means the cemetery, Molly," Emma said.

"Right. I knew that."

"Nigel rather fancies living next to a graveyard." Harriet poured the boiling water into the teapot, refilled the kettle, and switched it on again. "He plans to have it as the background of his author photo. On the book jacket."

"You'd also be living near a celebrity influencer," Emma said. "Jandie Brand and her husband are renting the house next door."

"Oh ah, now that you mention it, it's possible I've heard of her," Harriet said a little too casually. "It might be handy, mightn't it, to know an influencer when it comes time to publicize Nigel's book."

The electric kettle clicked off and Harriet filled the teapot for a second time, this time with the tea leaves in it. "He'll have to do it all himself, you know. Publishers don't lift a finger these days for their authors. Shocking, really."

"Jandie's missing, you know," Emma said.

"Missing?" Harriet brightened. "How exciting. Perhaps we should organize a search party."

"Listen, everyone," I said, "let's not go barging into their business. Maybe she doesn't want to be found."

"Maybe the husband's topped her," Harriet countered.

"That's what I think," Emma said.

"It's usually the husband," Pat agreed.

"She could be moldering under the floorboards right now," Harriet added cheerily as she came over and poured tea.

"Or he cut her into pieces and fed her to his fancy fish," Emma said.

"That's an angle," Pat said. "Ha! So to speak."

Emma socked him in the shoulder.

"Good one, Pat."

"Everyone, *please* do not harass the tenants," I pleaded. "The only reason they're here is because they wanted to live in a quiet neighborhood."

"Not much of a quiet neighborhood, is it?" Harriet handed me a brimming teacup. "What with everyone going round murdering each other."

CHAPTER ELEVEN

HARRIET PERSUADED US TO WALK UP THE STREET AND GIVE her our opinions on the house she was considering. The rain had started up again, so I handed out umbrellas from the spare-umbrella basket we keep by the front door. Emma and Pat each took one, but Harriet chose to walk under Pat's instead of taking one for herself.

The house Harriet was interested in looked very much like the other early twentieth-century plantation houses on the street. It had dark green vertical plank siding, white trim, and a corrugated red metal roof. It was on the same side of the street as my house, and like mine, it overlooked the cemetery. The drop-off from the backyard was a steep fifteen or twenty feet. We walked to the low retaining wall and looked out over the rolling lawn. It was vibrant green—no sprinklers required in Mahina—and dotted with glistening gravestones.

I caught a whiff of smoke. Harriet was puffing away on her pipe. I moved away to avoid breathing too much of it in. The smoke didn't seem to bother Pat, who was still sharing an umbrella with her. They were talking about something, but I couldn't hear over the sound of the rain pattering on my own umbrella.

I sidled back in close enough to hear the conversation.

"Easier to plant a hedge or something," Emma said. "You could do it yourself."

"Yeah, a landlord springing for an actual safety improvement?" Pat said. "What was I thinking?"

"Hey now," I said. "We're not all evil exploiters. Some of us try to take good care of our renters. Are you guys talking about the retaining wall?"

"Nigel and I won't be out here dancing on the precipice," Harriet assured us. "We've loads of space in the screened-in lanai."

"Ooh, screened-in lanai sounds nice," I said. "Imagine sitting outside without having to douse yourself in bug spray first."

"I never get bitten when I'm at your house," Emma said.

"Yeah, me neither," Pat added.

"That's because I'm there," I said, "and they're biting me and not you. Next time you guys can try sitting out there by yourselves."

"You must be giving off loads of carbon dioxide, Barda," Harriet said. "Best we keep moving then."

We followed Harriet and her trail of pipe smoke around the side of the house. Pat, who was by far the tallest member of our little party, tried to use his phone flashlight to peer into the windows, but the glass jalousies had a pebbled texture that made it impossible to see inside.

"So what do you think?" I asked Harriet as we headed back down the street. "It looks nice enough from the outside. I mean, if you want to live next to a cemetery, I know it's not for everyone. Moving is a big decision. Moving all your stuff and everything."

"Bit spendy, but worth it, I think. It's an investment in Nigel's career, after all. Someplace quiet to get his writing done. We do so want his book to be a success."

We were approaching my house when Harriet said this,

and I thought I saw her glance in the direction of my rental unit. Great. Add Harriet Holmes and her husband Nigel to the list of people who are going to be pestering me for an introduction to Jandie Brand.

"Well, it would certainly be delightful to have you as neighbors," I said. "Although I have to be honest. If you'd asked me last week, I would have said the neighborhood was safe. But now, with Jandie Brand disappeared? I don't know what to say."

"Oh, I expect it's not as bad as all that," Harriet said. "Nigel abducted by rabid fans? We should be so lucky, as the song says. Ah, here we are."

Harriet climbed onto her Triumph and roared off, calling back, "Cheerio!"

Pat, Emma, and I hosed off our muddy feet and left our footwear to dry on the front porch. Thanks to days of incessant rain, the atmosphere inside was close and damp. I cranked the ceiling fans up to top speed in an attempt to dry things out.

"An investment in Nigel's career. Did you hear her? This is about me getting them an audience with Jandie Brand." I headed into the kitchen to get two wine glasses. "Pat, help yourself to coffee or whatever you want to drink at this hour. Emma and I are having wine."

Emma hitched herself up to sit at the kitchen counter, and Pat took my invitation to make himself a cup of coffee."

"Wow, Harriet's a lot," Emma said. "I mean, I like her, but. Eh, you really think she's moving in to be close to Jandie?"

"I'm sure of it," I said. "Everyone seems to want to get close to Jandie. Even my friends, who I thought liked me for myself and enjoyed my company. Emma."

"Maybe this wasn't the right time for me to come visit." Pat finished fixing his coffee and took a seat next to Emma. "I mean for the sake of getting a story about her husband. Of course, it's always worth it to visit you guys. *I* enjoy your company, Molly."

Emma socked Pat in the shoulder. He laughed.

"Pat, I don't think Jandie's husband would mind talking to a reporter," Emma said. "I think he'd enjoy it. As long as the conversation is all about him and how smart he is. Eh, Pat, your mother never told you not to put your elbows on the table?"

Pat straightened up. "This is a counter, not a table. But whatever. I was surprised how much my editor loved the idea. Believe me, she doesn't love anything. Washed-up mainland celeb discovers the 'real' Hawaii and tries to reinvent himself, even as his young wife eclipses him and he realizes he'll never recapture even a fraction of his former fame and acclaim."

"Ouch." I handed over two furikake glasses to Emma, followed by the wine box. "It does sound like the kinds of depressing stories your paper likes to run, though."

"Yeah, it's right on brand for The Bleakly." Pat finished his coffee in one gulp. "Hey, you got any more of that tea? It was good."

"Sure, but I'm not sure I can replicate what Harriet did. You're welcome to try."

I traded places with Pat. He went into the kitchen to fill the electric kettle with tap water, and I sat down at the counter to fill myself with grocery-store cabernet.

"Is Mahina water still as good as it used to be?" Pat asked.

"Of course it is," Emma said. "Not like your nasty Honolulu water,"

"I liked meeting Harriet," Pat said. "I think she'd be fun to have as a neighbor."

"It might be," I said. "If I weren't her department chair. Wait a minute. Pat, you have a crush on Harriet?"

"Maybe a little one."

"You know she's married, right?" I said.

"Obviously, to someone named Nigel." Pat checked the

oven clock and poured boiling water into his cup. "Don't worry, it's completely chaste and above board. You have to admit, there's something about her."

"Maybe it's the 'posh' accent," I said. "The students seem to be bewitched by it. Even when she says things that would normally be super-offensive, I only get one or two complaints at most."

"Could be the pipe," Emma said. "How many women do you know who smoke a pipe?"

"I don't know anyone who smokes a pipe besides her," I said. "And for the record I do not find it charming. It's a constant battle trying to get her to comply with the on-campus smoking ban. Enforcement of which is my thankless responsibility, by the way. Somehow it always slips her mind that she's not allowed to smoke in the building. 'Oh dreadfully sorry Barda, made a bollocks out of it again haven't I,' and then I can't even be mad at her because she seems genuinely contrite even though I know she's not."

"So you're having fun being department chair?" Pat brought his tea over and joined us at the counter. "Hey, by the way. I invited someone to come by. I hope that's okay."

"Come by where?" I said. "Here? To my house?"

"The places downtown we'd normally meet are closed because of the flood warning. He's going to be here in..." Pat glanced at me and something in my expression must have motivated him to add, "Sorry, I can call and cancel."

"It depends," I said. "Who is it?"

"His name is Howell. He's a nice kid, writes for the *County Courier*."

CHAPTER TWELVE

"Pat, you invited a stranger into my house?"

I sped into the kitchen and started flinging dirty dishes into the dishwasher.

"Don't worry, your house looks fine," Pat said.

"No it doesn't, you huge liar. But it will. Can you clear all the stuff off the coffee table? Just bring it in here. I'll figure out what to do with it later. Why on earth are you helping someone from the *County Courier* anyway?"

"Why shouldn't I?" Pat asked.

"Because the *County Courier* laid you off, along with all the other decent reporters, and now they're basically a collection of ads for car dealers and furniture stores? Where did Emma go?"

"I'm in the bathroom," came a disembodied voice. "Don't talk to me."

"He's trying to get a start on his career and I want to help him out." Pat brought over an armload of coffee cups and junk mail and dumped everything on the counter next to the sink. "Good karma, pay it forward, and all that nonsense."

"It's very nice of you." I popped a detergent pod in the dishwasher, pushed the door shut, and got the cycle started. "I was thinking you were maybe cultivating him as an unwitting source, or doing some Machiavellian 'keep your friends close but your rivals closer' kind of thing. Darn it, there are still all these dirty cups. I'll have to wash them by hand."

"Here, I'll do it." Pat got up, filled the sink with soapy water, and swept the dishes into the sink. "There. Now you can't see them under the bubbles. Molly, you don't seem thrilled about Howell coming over. I thought you'd be interested in meeting a reporter. You always like hearing the village gossip."

"I do. But not when I'm in the middle of it. Pat, you came over to do a piece on a formerly-famous cartoonist. Okay, fine. But now his celebrity wife has disappeared and you just invited over a reporter from the local paper?"

"Sorry, Molly, like I said, I can call him and cancel."

"No, then he's going to ask you why and it's just going to seem like we're hiding something and it's going to turn into this big murder case. How am I going to explain this to Donnie? What if he sees it in the newspaper while he's over on the mainland? Things always sound worse when they make it onto the national news. Remember that story about the eruption, where they claimed the lava flowed all the way to Honolulu?"

"I wouldn't worry about getting your name dragged into this story, Molly. Look, I really appreciate you letting me do this. I didn't realize it was gonna cause so much stress."

Emma came out of the bathroom, wiping her hands on the back of her jeans.

"Eh, the place looks good," she said.

"I guess it does look okay. Thanks for helping me tidy up, Pat." I sat back down at the kitchen counter and refilled my wine glass. "I've been a little stressed out about this Senior Seminar thing."

"Oh, the business planning class?" Emma hitched herself up next to me and filled her own glass.

"Is that the class they called BP?" Pat asked.

"Yes. They still call it that. Anyway, you know Victor Santiago, the fundraising guy whose title I keep forgetting? Big Head Cheese of Money Raising or whatever he's called?"

"Vice-President for Student Outreach and Community Relations," Emma said.

"How on earth do you remember that, Emma? Anyway, my business planning students have a command performance at the Senior Showcase. You know the end-of-the-year dog and pony show where they invite all our VIP donors and Friends in the Business Community? This year Jerry Mizuno is going to be there. They've been trying to cultivate the Mizuno family for years. Victor told me this is probably our most important Senior Showcase ever. With the latest budget cuts from the ledge, we're more dependent than ever on private donations. He made sure I knew that he will not tolerate a repeat of what happened last year with the theater majors."

"So what's the problem?" Emma asked. "I mean, I don't think your business students are gonna put on pig masks and critique capitalism through poetry and burlesque."

"No, thankfully. But Victor wants to project a proper, dignified image of our school. My students are just turning in their first drafts now, and, well, the best plan by far is for something called Party Pooper."

"What is it?" Pat asked.

"It's a handheld device meant to carry in your pocket or purse. It's a combination noisemaker and deodorizer dispenser, for when you're away from home and nature calls."

"Eh, sounds like a great idea," Emma said. "Tell me when they start selling it. I'll buy a bunch for the next time Yoshi has his paddler friends over to our house."

"This is Jerry Mizuno as in Mizuno Mart?" Pat asked. "I mean, Mizuno Mart sells toilet paper and stuff like that. I don't see how your Party Pooper product is gonna offend them."

"I don't know. I hope you're right."

"Molly, at least they're coming up with their own ideas," Emma said. "Count your blessings, ah? Remember last year when I found a bunch of my students buying their homework solutions online?"

"What did you end up doing about that?" Pat asked.

"No more research papers or homework. Nothing you could pay someone to do for you. I'm only assigning in-class exams and presentations now."

"How does that work in your online classes?" I asked.

"A hundred percent of the grade is oral exams. There's no hiding it if you don't know the material. Really separates the wheat from the chaff."

"Ouch," I said. "I can't imagine the Student Retention Office is happy about that. Their whole mission is No Chaff Left Behind."

"Yeah, well, no big loss there. I'm already on the Student Retention Office's 'Party Pooper' list. But the good part is, the students who make it through my class? They know their stuff now, when they go on to the higher level classes. You know da kine, who teaches anatomy and physiology? She's ready to name her firstborn after me."

We were interrupted by a quick knock.

"That's him." Pat jumped up and bounded to the front door.

"What was his name?" I asked.

"Howell," Pat said. "Howard Howell."

Howell looked to be in his mid-twenties, with auburn hair and a friendly, freckled face. He wore typical Mahina business attire, an aloha shirt tucked into slacks, but he struck me as not being local.

Great, I thought. *I've turned into one of those provincial small-towners who sizes people up and decides they're "not from around here."*

"Call me Howdy." The young man reached out and grasped my hand. His flat Midwestern accent confirmed that he was not, in fact, "from around here." And his gap-toothed grin forever cemented in my mind his resemblance to Howdy Doody.

We were all standing around awkwardly now, so I invited everyone to sit in the living room.

"I'll make coffee." Pat headed into the kitchen.

"Decaf for me if you don't mind," Howdy called after him, "thank you Mr. Flanagan!"

"I'll do decaf for everyone. It's easier."

I wished Pat had let me make the coffee so I wouldn't have to make conversation with this complete stranger, but at least Emma was there with me.

"I'll go put together some snacks," Emma said, and got up and disappeared into the kitchen.

Fortunately Howdy Howell was good at keeping conversation afloat. When he found out I taught in the College of Commerce at Mahina State, he asked how I liked working in the repurposed Inebriates' Asylum, and did I think it was haunted? I replied that I liked the old building very much, and I half-hoped it was haunted as I would love to meet the ghost of the Inebriates' Asylum founder, Constance Brigham. The spirit of the eccentric heiress was rumored to roam the old hospital complex.

"I was surprised to find out Mahina had its own university," Howdy said. "I don't mean anything bad by it. Nothing at all wrong with small towns, I always say. I cover high school sports for the *County Courier*, and let me tell you, it's just like back home. People sure do love their high school football."

"Our university get football too." Emma came into the living room and set down a tray of goodies. "Go Fighting Moons."

I supposed I could forgive Emma for abandoning me. She

had pulled together whatever snack-like items she could find in my kitchen, including nuts, tortilla chips, and some long-forgotten chocolate buttons that had developed a white bloom.

Pat came out holding four pre-poured cups of coffee and handed them around.

"You notice they're the *Fighting* Moons, not the *Winning* Moons," he said. "At least with the high school teams you got a chance. Hey Howdy, did you tell her about the story you're doing?"

"Story?" I looked from Pat to Howdy and back.

"He kind of beat me to the punch," Pat said. "He's doing a story on your tenants. The influencer and the has-been."

CHAPTER THIRTEEN

"WHAT?" I NEARLY DROPPED MY COFFEE CUP. "LOOK, PAT, Howdy, I'm sorry, I can't be party to violating my tenants' privacy. When they signed their lease, they were very clear—"

Howdy blushed.

"Oh golly no, Professor Barda, it's not like that. I'm not invading anyone's privacy. In fact, Jandie reached out to me."

"It turns out they're fine with publicity," Pat said. "On their own terms, of course."

"Emma," I asked, "did you know about this?"

Emma shook her head.

"But if they wanna talk to someone, you can't stop 'em, right?"

"Anyone can talk to whomever they like," I said. "I just feel like an idiot standing up for their privacy this whole time."

"Nah, you're doing the right thing," Emma said. "Screen out the riff-raff. But maybe you don't have to be so *farbissen* with your friends."

"It's a great story," Howdy said. "Celebrity couple moves to the middle of nowhere, they find inner strength they didn't know they had. They rediscover themselves and their love for each other."

FRANKIE BOW

"The middle of *nowhere?*" Emma glared at Howdy. "The celebrity couple slumming it with us backwards country bumpkins? Is that what you're going with?"

"No, no, not at all, Professor Nakamura. It's only, that's how Mr. Ladd..." Howie ran his hand through his already-unruly ginger hair. "Mr. Ladd called it the middle of nowhere. But I'm sure he means it in a good way."

Emma pointed her stubby forefinger at Howdy.

"Well, you tell him he's wrong. Mahina's the biggest town on the island. We get paved roads, county water, and we're connected to the electrical grid. Some of us even get sewer hookup. It's not like we're down in Kuewa."

"Way to convince him we're not a backwater, Emma," I said.

"You're right, Professor Nakamura," Howdy said cheerfully. "I actually have been to Kuewa. I know exactly what you're talking about. Jandie took me down there, to show me where they were originally thinking of settling down. They liked how affordable it was. But she needs good internet so that was a dealbreaker for her. Professor Barda, what do you think about Jandie and Mr. Ladd? Are they as perfect a couple as they seem?"

"I try not to talk about people behind their backs," I said.

Pat snorted, which I thought was extremely uncalled-for.

"Sure, I understand. Say, I have another question, did any of you happen to see Jandie today?"

Emma and I exchanged a glance.

"No, not today, that I recall," I said cautiously. "Why?"

"I was supposed to have an interview with her this morning, but she wasn't at home."

"She didn't share her plans with me," I said. "Oh look, we're getting low on coffee. Emma, can you help me find the new coffee I just bought?"

Emma followed me into the kitchen. We ducked into the mud room, and out to the lanai. From there we had a view of

64

the rental house and the cemetery, quiet under the
green-gray sky.

"Jandie Brand missed an appointment with a reporter this
morning," I said. "What social media personality does that?
The husband's already told us he's worried about her.
Something is weird here."

"The husband is what's weird. If anyone did something
shady, it's him. Eh, I got another question. You think he calls
himself Howdy to mess with people cause he knows he looks
like Howdy Doody?"

"I was wondering the same thing! I didn't know you knew
what Howdy Doody looked like."

"Only cause of that weird hipster t-shirt you have that says
it's Howdy Doody time, whatever that means."

Emma hoisted herself up and perched on the railing.

"Don't worry," she said, "I'm not gonna fall down. I get
excellent balance from paddling."

"I'm still not joining your paddling crew. Nice try though.
Okay, about this situation. What should we do? Should we tell
her husband about the missed appointment?"

"Not if he's the reason she's missing."

"You don't trust him."

"Molly, do you?"

"No, not really. You know this is the first time in his adult
life that Donnie's taken a vacation. He trusted me to hold
everything together while he was traveling. Won't he be
surprised when he comes back to a house of chaos and
murder."

"Jandie getting murdered by her husband isn't your fault,
Molly."

"What if nothing's changed by the time Donnie and the
baby get back, and now poor little Francesca's living next door
to a murderer? Emma, what should I do?"

"What, you're gonna let him stay here after he murdered
his wife?"

65

FRANKIE BOW

"No, of course not. But the only alternative is I'd have to evict a murderer. We're just going to have to move, that's all."

"You should go back inside," Emma said.

"Yeah, you're right. I'm being a bad hostess. Wait, what do you mean *I* should go back inside? Where are you going?"

"I gotta go pick up the mail and check on my idiot brother and my doofus husband."

"Okay. Well, send them my love. Sounds like they need it."

Pat and Howdy were still talking when I went back inside. I didn't have the energy to reinsert myself into the conversation, so I went into my bedroom to check my email. There was a new message from Donnie, with a photo. Donnie was holding Francesca in front of a scaled-down Eiffel Tower. They had made it to Vegas. Francesca was beaming. She looked bigger than when I'd seen her last—was that possible? Donnie was unshaven and looked exhausted.

I missed Donnie and Francesca. I wouldn't even have minded visiting Donnie's grandson, Davison Hiapo Keali'i Gonsalves Balusteros (aka Junior). Junior was a little older than Francesca and was technically her nephew. But I was happy to keep my distance from Junior's father (and my stepson), Davison Gonsalves. Davison had been my student once upon a time. In my years of teaching at Mahina State, I've had many wonderful students whom I remember with fondness. Davison is not one of them.

I wrote back telling Donnie I missed them and wished I could be there with them. Now, how much news to share? Donnie had enough to worry about, traveling with the baby. There was no point in telling him things that were just going to stress him out.

"Donnie, our renter disappeared, and we think her husband murdered her! Or maybe a deranged fan did her in. There's probably hundreds of those skulking around!" No, that wouldn't do.

CHAPTER FOURTEEN

DONNIE WOULD WANT TO KNOW WHETHER THERE HAD BEEN any hurricane damage. I wrote that the bottom of Uakoko Street had flooded temporarily, but our property was safely out of harm's way. I told him Pat and Emma had both come to visit, so he didn't have to worry about my being alone in the house. He would be amused to hear that Harriet Holmes' husband Nigel had apparently gotten a publisher interested in his memoir about the time he'd spent in prison for protesting a tree-felling scheme in his neighborhood. I sent my sincere love and best wishes to the Davisons, père et fils. I wasn't sure whether Junior's mom Tiffany was still in the picture so be on the safe side, I didn't mention her.

What else? Oh, of course, food. I told him how much I was enjoying all the food from the Drive-Inn that Donnie had left in the freezer. And that the aunties had mobbed me at St. Damien's yesterday, telling me they couldn't wait until Donnie's Drive-Inn reopened so that they could once again walk over and enjoy their after-Mass coffee.

I pressed "send" and was about to go back into the living room and pretend to be a good hostess, when I saw a notification pop up in my in-box.

A submission had been uploaded to the Business Planning class. I clicked over to see what else had been turned in. Something that would wow our potential donors and compel them to open their wallets, I hoped. Or at least something that would appease Victor Santiago, Lord High Inquisitor of Community Connections or whatever the heck his title was.

The proposed product was a deodorizing spray for pet accidents. Not particularly innovative, but overall a solid business idea.

I read through the outline of the plan. Other than the product name possibly causing Victor Santiago's monocle to drop into his teacup, it looked fine. In fact, it was quite good. A huge improvement on the student's previous work, almost as if it were written by a different...

Oh no.

I was already stressed out enough about the Senior Showcase. Now I had to deal with plagiarism on top of everything else.

I downloaded the paper to my computer and uploaded it into the plagiarism checking site. Nothing popped out. I wanted to believe this was the student's own work, and he had simply been inspired to his highest levels of performance by my exceptional teaching.

Yeah, right. I'm as prone to self-serving bias as the next person, but I'm not delusional.

I had done everything I was supposed to do to avoid plagiarism. Design unique assignments that can't be found online. Have students turn in consecutive drafts instead of having one big paper due at the end of the semester. But none of it helps if the student is paying someone else to do the assignments.

I called Emma. She didn't pick up, so I left a message and went through the rest of my email. I hoped by the time I emerged from my bedroom, Howdy would be gone.

Howdy stood up when I entered the living room.

"Thanks so much for your hospitality, Professor Barda," he said. "I'm going to get going now. Thanks for everything, Mr. Flanagan."

"I'm gonna call it a day," Pat said when Howdy was gone.

"Pat, was he waiting for me?"

"Yeah, he didn't want to be rude and leave without saying goodbye. Okay, good night. Hey, thanks for letting me stay over."

"I figured your independent weekly wasn't exactly going to put you up at the Hanohano Hotel," I said.

"You got that right. They didn't even cover my plane fare." Pat yawned and sauntered off to the guest room.

I was still clearing off the coffee table when I heard a sharp knock on the front door, followed by someone jiggling the knob.

"Hang on Emma, I'll be right there."

When I opened the door, Emma sped past me and made a beeline to the kitchen. She filled two furikake glasses with wine, and plunked them down on the counter.

"I got your message. So you got an essay mill situation going in your class, ah?"

"Maybe. I was hoping you could help me figure it out, since you've dealt with this before. Hey, how's everything at home? Is your house still standing?"

"Barely. I don't wanna talk about it. Eh, you don't know how to repair drywall, do you?"

"Me? Of course not. Pat might, though. Ask him tomorrow, he's already out for the night."

"Pat went out? Where? What's open on Monday night besides the Pair-O-Dice? Oh no Molly, it's open mic improv night at the Pair-O-Dice. We gotta stop him."

"I meant he's 'out' as in out like a light. He's asleep."

"Oh. Yeah, that makes sense. So what's the assignment you think is plagiarized?"

FRANKIE BOW

I set my laptop on the counter in front of Emma. She squinted at the screen.

"Urine Luck?"

"That's the product name."

"Oh, I see. 'Looking for a solution to smelly household accidents? Urine luck.' That's kinda clever."

Emma sat up and turned to me.

"Almost *too* clever," she added.

"Exactly! See what I mean?"

"How's it compare to the student's other work?"

"Very different," I said. "It's like he vaulted ahead ten grade levels in half a semester. Plus the SWOT analysis is flawless."

"The what analysis?" Emma asked.

"Strengths, Weaknesses, Opportunities, Threats. SWOT."

Emma sat back and folded her arms.

"Hmm. Yeah, definitely suspicious. You should have 'em come into your office and explain it to you."

"What if it really is his own work, though? It'll look like I'm falsely accusing him."

"Eh, you're letting the Student Retention Office get inside your head now. Know what, I got some pre-meds in my class I can talk to. If there's anyone who knows more about cheating than your business majors do, it's the pre-meds. Lemme ask around. Eh, I got some news for you, Molly. Know how come I was able to get over here so fast after you called? I was checking out the house."

"Checking out what house?" I asked.

"I think you need more wine. I'm just gonna bring the box over."

"Emma, I'm not even done with the glass you just gave me. What house? What is going on?"

Emma plunked the wine box on the counter and hitched herself up onto the bar stool next to me.

"I got back here about an hour ago."

70

"You've been here the whole time?" I asked.

"Yeah. I noticed Edward Ladd's big stupid overcompensating truck wasn't there. So I figured I'd go inside and check it out."

"Inside the rental unit? That's breaking and entering!"

"No it's not," Emma retorted. "You're the owner, you have something in your contract that lets you go inside any time, right?"

"Well, yeah, I do. But you went in, not me."

"So you gave me permission."

"Emma, I did not—"

"I was acting on your behalf to check on the well-being of the occupants."

I should have been angry at Emma for going into the house without permission. But I was too curious to be mad.

"Whatever. Where did he go? Do you think he went out to look for Jandie?"

Emma shrugged.

"Maybe he went out to check where he hid the body."

"So what did you find?" I asked.

Emma took an infuriatingly long draught of wine.

"Her bed was messy."

"Is that unusual?" I asked.

"It is for Jandie. On camera it's always perfect."

Emma handed me her phone. The screen showed a photo from Jandie Brand's account. Pink-and-white ruffled throw pillows were perfectly placed on a smooth, sugar-pink bedspread. The window framed a sunny day outside, and the soft-focus background filter was cranked up so far that the graveyard in the background looked like a gauzy meadow.

"You know," I said, "it's possible that in real life her room doesn't always look as perfect as it does on camera. Emma, what would you have said if someone walked in and caught you snooping around Jandie's bedroom?"

"I woulda told 'em you authorized me to be there."

71

"Great. So aside from a messy bed, did you actually find anything?"

"Nah, but I wasn't in there that long. I was just seeing if there was something obvious, like a dead body in the freezer or something. Eh, thanks for not getting too mad about it."

I set down my empty wine glass.

"No, Emma, you bring up a good point. I am allowed to go in and inspect the unit. It's in the contract. Maybe I should go have a look."

"Whoa, wait, Molly, what?"

I slid off the chair and stood tall, quickly grabbing the edge of the counter for balance. I had skipped dinner, so two glasses of wine may have packed more of a punch than usual. I wasn't afraid at all. In fact I was brimming with courage and curiosity.

"I'm going, Emma. You can't stop me."

"Hey, don't go without me." Emma drained her glass and followed me out to the cold, dark yard.

CHAPTER FIFTEEN

THE CHILLY NIGHT AIR HAD A SOBERING EFFECT. BY THE TIME we were at the door of the rental unit I wanted to turn around and go back home. But I couldn't, not with Emma right there.

The floor plan of the rental unit was a scaled-down, mirror image of the main house. Which meant the carport was to my left...this was so confusing.

"Emma, you should take the lead," I said. "You already did the, you know. Reconsaponce...responkabonk...pre-looking."

"Reconnaissance?" Emma said.

"Yes! That's what I said."

Maybe the cold night air hadn't been that sobering after all.

I followed Emma as she moved seemingly at random from one spot to the next, opening drawers, sticking her arm down between the bed and the wall, and crawling along the baseboard.

"Emma," I said, "you're like a human Roomba. Just bouncing around."

"The Roomba algorithm works," Emma retorted, from underneath the bed. As she was backing out, she kicked over a wastebasket. I righted it, thankful that it was empty. Then I saw a hot pink sticky note stuck to the inside. I quickly plucked the piece of paper from the wastebasket and pocketed it. Realizing I had just touched a stranger's garbage, I ducked into the bathroom and washed my hands for a solid sixty seconds.

We covered the rest of the small dwelling quickly but didn't find anything out of place. Jandie had a reflector set up next to the window in the third bedroom, so she was probably using that as her photo studio.

"See?" I said to Emma. "She doesn't even sleep here. That bed is just a prop. This room is her photo studio."

"Maybe she does sleep here," Emma retorted. "You don't know where Jandie sleeps."

I went over to the bed and knocked on it. It was hard, and made a hollow sound. I lifted up the pink bedspread to expose plywood.

"So she sleeps on plywood," Emma retorted. "That's not a crime. What's your point?"

"I forget."

We looked through the rest of the house, paying particular attention to the freezer (which contained a half-empty carton of strawberry cheesecake ice cream and nothing else).

Finally we decided we had conducted as thorough a search as possible under the circumstances and decided to head back to the main house.

"So what do you think?" I asked Emma as we squelched across the wet lawn. The rain was starting up again, so we walked faster.

"Nothing really looked out of place," Emma said. "Although we can't be sure that nothing's missing, cause we don't know what was there before."

"Well, there were no suspicious odors or loose floorboards," I said. "That's something."

"Eh Molly, what if the husband doesn't come back? What if they're both missing? What about your rent?"

"They paid the six-month lease in advance," I said.

"Aha! Now I'm thinking maybe *you* whacked 'em."

"Hilarious."

Did they have two cars or just one?" Emma asked.

"I've only ever seen the big black truck that the husband drives. I think Jandie takes the Sampan when she needs to go somewhere."

"Oh yeah, that's right. She get a lotta posts with her riding in the Sampan."

When we got back to my house Pat was awake, relaxing in the living room and drinking coffee.

"If you want to know anything about their private life, you could just ask Howdy," Pat said.

"What?" Emma said.

"Howdy Howell. The reporter. He's interviewed them a few times now. He'd be happy to talk to you."

"What are you talking about?" I asked innocently.

"I'm talking about your tenants, whose house you two were just snooping around in."

"Shame on you spying on us!" Emma said.

"I wasn't spying. I saw you through the window, coming out of their front door."

"I'm the landlady," I said. "I have the right to inspect the house. It's in the contract."

"What were you looking for anyway?"

"Jandie," Emma said.

"What, you mean you were looking for her dead body?"

"No," Emma said

"Maybe," I said at the same time. "Oh! Pat. I just remembered something I was wondering about. Why did Tedd Ladd stop drawing? He was doing his cartoon, he was super popular, and then he just stopped. He never explained why."

"I asked Howdy the same thing," Pat said. Emma and I plunked down on either side of him on the couch.

"And then?" Emma prompted him.

"Probably just grief," Pat said. "It happened around when his first wife passed away."

"His first wife died, ah?" Emma stood and went to the front window. Outside, sheets of rain, illuminated by my porch light, glinted in the dark. "So was it really grief? Or guilt?"

CHAPTER SIXTEEN

"LADD'S FIRST WIFE DIED OF CANCER." PAT GOT UP FROM THE couch and went into the kitchen to fix himself a cup of coffee. "But sure, Emma, accuse a grieving widower of murder."

"I hope they're not on the road right now," I said. "Pitch dark, hard rain. Not a good combination."

Our rural island had few streetlights, and the ones we did have were deliberately kept dim to minimize any light pollution that might interfere with the telescopes.

"I have Jandie's cell phone number," I said. "Should I call her?"

"You have her cell number?" Emma whirled around to glare at me. "How come you never called her when she went missing?"

"Sorry, I didn't think of it. Okay, I'm calling her now."

I dialed Jandie's number, but I got an "all circuits are busy" message. Same thing on the second try.

"I should have tried her phone before," I said. "I think I should call the police. Her husband said he was going to, but I don't trust him. If they yell at me for being a nuisance, fine. I'd rather that than know I could've done something and didn't."

"It's possible you're overreacting," Emma said. "But I wouldn't bet Jandie's life on it."

"I agree, you've already annoyed the police as much as anyone possibly could," Pat added helpfully.

"Oh yeah, remember that time they had to mobilize every emergency vehicle on the island to find her?" Emma said. "I thought Detective Da Kine was gonna blow a gasket."

"That unfortunate situation was not my fault, and you both know it." I called the non-emergency police line and left a message describing the situation. I honestly didn't expect to hear back. But to my amazement, not ten minutes later a police cruiser pulled up in front of my house.

I opened my door.

"...Detective Medeiros?"

The detective was broadly built, and tall enough to hit his head on my door frame if he didn't duck. His thick black hair was tied back in a ponytail and he had a small goatee. He wore a colorful, presumably custom-tailored aloha shirt (I don't think they're available off-the-rack in his size).

But something was different about Detective Medeiros. Had he gotten new tattoos? A haircut?

"Aloha." He put out a beefy hand. I hesitated. The friendly gesture was way out of character for Detective Ka`imi Medeiros, whose attitude toward me ranged from annoyance to exasperation.

"Detective Brian Medeiros," the man said. "You called about your tenant, Jandie Brand?"

"Oh! *Brian* Medeiros. I thought you were—"

"Yeah, I get that a lot. Ka`imi is my cousin. He's the brains of the family. I'm the handsome one."

"Ah!"

"May I come in?"

"What? Oh. Yes. Yes, of course! Thank you for coming so quickly. Please."

I led him into the living room and introduced Pat and Emma, who gawked at him rather rudely, in my opinion. They hadn't heard our exchange and were clearly shocked to see Detective Medeiros being so cordial.

I, too, wondered what had earned me this VIP treatment, but I wasn't going to question it. No need to bite the hand of the gift horse that feeds me, as poor Jandie would say.

"I'm so glad you came," I said. "The thing is, I'm worried about my renters. They're kind of new here, and they went out just as the bad weather is coming in. I can't reach them by phone."

"Lucky for your tenants, the mayor has a personal interest in their well-being," Medeiros eased down onto the opposite end of the couch from me. I felt my side of the couch lift until my feet dangled above the floor.

"The *mayor?*" Pat, Emma, and I exclaimed at once.

"Does the mayor know them personally?" I asked.

"Not yet. I think he'd appreciate an introduction, but. The wahine, not the husband."

"Good choice," Emma said. "So our mayor's a Jandista?"

"What is that?" Medeiros asked.

"Someone who's a fan of Jandie Brand," Emma said.

Medeiros looked pained.

"In a way, I suppose you could say. But it's not about her music or whatever."

"There's no music involved," Pat said. "She's an influencer. Famous for being famous."

Medeiros heaved a sigh.

"Okay, the thing about it is, Jandie Brand is making Mahina look like a real appealing destination with all her photos and da kine that she puts up. She's been good for our economy."

"So it's about tourist dollars," Pat said. "Sorry, I mean *visitor* dollars."

"More importantly, yen, yuan, and euros," Medeiros said. "The international visitors spend more. If something happens to Jandie Brand, it's bad for our restaurants and hotels and da kine. Anyway, that's probably more than you needed to know."

"No, thank you for giving us that background," I said. "It's very helpful."

As a naturally inquisitive person, I appreciated the detective's openness. Detective Brian Medeiros's cousin, Detective Ka'imi Medeiros, always acted like he'd get his pay docked if he dared to give me any information.

Detective Medeiros went on to ask all of us the expected questions about the missing couple, and some unexpected ones as well. What was my relationship with the tenants, did I get along with them, were they having money problems, had I noticed unusual behavior from the neighbors?

My warm feelings toward the "good" Detective Medeiros (as I now thought of him) cooled a bit when I noticed his questions becoming unnecessarily repetitive, as if he were trying to catch one of us out in a lie. Or perhaps some sin of omission. Like omitting the fact that Emma and I had been snooping in the rental house.

Unfortunately, his method turned out to be effective.

"You entered their *house?*" Medeiros looked from me to Emma and back, not bothering to conceal his surprise. "Both of you? When they wasn't there?"

"She went first," I said.

"Yeah, well she came in afterwards an' helped."

"Blaming each other isn't gonna work," Pat said. "You're both getting kicked out of paradise."

"We didn't do anything wrong, Detective Medeiros. It's *my* house." Even to myself I sounded whiny and defensive. "According to the lease I can inspect it at any time."

"Do you go into your tenants' house regularly?" Medeiros asked.

"Well...no. This was the first time."

"Why today then?"

"The same reason we called you," I said. "Because they're missing and we're worried about them. Oh, and they were supposed to meet someone and missed the appointment. Pat, your friend Howdy, I can't think of his real last name."

"Howdy Howell," Pat said. "Yeah, that's true."

"I'll need his contact information from you." Medeiros turned to Emma. "Did you remove anything from the house?"

She shook her head.

"You?" He turned to me.

"No, I didn't...oh, hang on."

I remembered the sticky note I'd found stuck to the inside of the trash can. I dug it out of my bag and held it out to Pat.

"Why are you giving this to me?" Pat asked.

"You have your phone out. Take a picture. Please."

Pat snapped the picture and handed the paper back to me. I leaned across the couch and handed it to Medeiros. He glanced at it, folded it in half, and stuck it in his shirt pocket.

"You shouldn't have removed anything from the house," he said.

"That note was in the trash."

"Is the house a crime scene?" Emma asked.

"Is it?" I asked.

Medeiros braced his hands on his knees and stood. My side of the couch thunked back down to earth.

"Not that we know of. I'm going to go check it out right now. Will you be here in case I have any more questions?"

We assured him we would.

As soon as he was gone, I heaved a sigh of relief.

"What a day." I went into the kitchen to check whether the rice in the rice cooker was still good. It was fine, maybe a little hard around the edges. "How many people did I have to interact with? Edward Ladd, Harriet Holmes, Howdy Doo—Howdy Howell, Detective Medeiros 2.0."

"What about me and Emma?" Pat asked.

"You guys don't count. It's strangers and acquaintances that wear me out. You're the kind of friends I can ask to set the table while I heat up dinner. Oh yeah, anyone else up for a late dinner? I'm famished."

CHAPTER SEVENTEEN

"I LIKE THIS DETECTIVE MEDEIROS BETTER," EMMA SAID
through a mouthful of kim chee chili and rice. "The other one
is so uptight."

"It's because Molly's a landlord now," Pat said. "Of course
the police are gonna be nice to her. The agents of class control
work for the oppressor class."

"Oh, *I'm* an oppressor now? Pat, you're the one who's
always saying individual choices don't matter within the
context of a capitalist system. Besides, I thought you said you
liked the rental unit."

"I do like it," Pat said. "I'm not judging, I'm just
observing."

"Speaking of people judging me," I said, "I still can't
figure out why Jandie Brand called me a crackpot."

"She what?" Pat asked.

"We went over to their house to warn them about the
hurricane," Emma said. "We overheard 'em talking, and
Jandie was saying what about the landlady, she has trouble
minding her own business and she's kind of a crackpot."

"You can't argue the point about minding your business,"

Pat said. "You only heard her say it because you were eavesdropping at the time."

A knock on the door interrupted the conversation.

"I'll get it." Emma hopped up and opened the door to Detective Medeiros.

"Eh, Detective, you like come in?"

"No, I just wanted to let you know I'm leaving now."

"You find anything suspicious?" Emma asked.

"If you see anything unusual, call and let me know. You can leave a message if there's no answer."

Medeiros handed his card to Emma and left.

We cleaned up and Pat disappeared into the guest room. Emma and I agreed that it wasn't a good idea for her to drive on such a dark and stormy night. Well, maybe not exactly stormy, but it was drizzling. And the cloud cover definitely made it dark.

Emma got comfortable on the living room couch and called Yoshi to tell him she was staying with me. She launched into a narrative of the day's events, starting with our visit to the rental unit and Edward Ladd's admission that his wife was missing. There didn't seem to be any harm in it. Medeiros hadn't sworn us to secrecy or anything, and I supposed Yoshi must be as eager for news as anyone. Even more so, in fact, because Yoshi loved being the expert and the first to know things. This quirk of his was amusing at a distance and really annoying otherwise. I flipped the porch light on and went to bed.

The rain was so loud on the metal roof I had trouble falling asleep. The instant I did, or so it seemed, I was awakened by a banging on the front door.

Now what? I walked by the couch and shook Emma awake, and then we both tiptoed to the front door. I put my eye to the peephole.

Harriet Holmes was standing on my front porch, calmly shaking the water off her umbrella. I opened the door and quickly hustled her inside, glancing around to see who might have been pursuing her.

No one was.

No, it just happened that in Harriet Holmes's mind, ten o'clock at night in the hammering rain seemed like a perfectly appropriate time for a neighborly visit.

Before I knew it she was in my kitchen. She pulled out three matching furikake glasses from the dishwasher.

"I wouldn't have popped round," Harriet said, "only I saw you had your light on. Cheers. Or should I say, *sláinte*. Speaking of which, where's young Flanagan?"

"Asleep in the guest room," I said. "He can sleep through anything. Evidently."

Harriet sat at the dining table and placed the glasses down. From somewhere within the various pockets and folds of her battered field coat, she produced a full-sized bottle of whiskey and set it on the table.

"Whoa, nice!" Emma hurried into the kitchen. "I'm gonna get the Chicken Boy mug. Molly, are the dishes clean?"

"In the dishwasher? Yes. I ran it this afternoon. Emma, what's wrong with the furikake glasses?"

"Nothing, I just like Chicken Boy."

The furikake glasses hold about six ounces. The Chicken Boy mug has about three times that capacity.

"Oh yeah, still warm," Emma said as she retrieved the mug. "Eh Harriet, you make a decision on the place up the street?"

"We did," Harriet said. "Nigel and I went round and signed the lease this afternoon. It's official. We're neighbors."

Emma and I joined Harriet at the table. She pulled off the top of the bottle and poured us each a generous amount.

"That's great news, Harriet, welcome to the neighborhood." I raised my glass halfway and set it down. I so dearly wanted to be back in bed at this point, I didn't even have the energy to drink.

"You decided you rather have a view of the cemetery?" Emma asked.

"Mm." Harriet sipped her whiskey. "Be a welcome change, to be honest. Clyde, he's my landlord you know, he's been rather a dry stick ever since Nigel's come to Mahina."

Harriet still pronounced it "Ma-HIGH-na." I'd tried correcting her a few times, but it never stuck. I eventually gave up.

"Oh yeah, I get it," Emma said.

"I expected Clyde and Nigel to get on," Harriet said, "They've so much in common. They both have a bit of the outlaw about them, haven't they?"

I didn't see the similarity myself. Nigel Holmes was a retired law professor, the kind of person who would wander around for an hour looking for his glasses only to realize they've been perched on his forehead the whole time. Clyde Hamamoto, on the other hand, had the insignia of his motorcycle club tattooed on his neck.

"But when it comes down to it," Harriet was saying, "Clyde can be appallingly conventional, never mind the plaited beard and the leather waistcoat and all the rest of it. Bit of a disappointment, really. I say, on the topic of rentals, Barda, there's been a bit of activity around yours, what?"

"Detective Medeiros come by today," Emma said. "Looks like the mayor's taking Jandie's disappearance seriously, so Mahina PD is too. Molly and me, we think the husband killed her."

"We do not necessarily think that, Emma" I countered. "Oh, sorry, Harriet, please no smoking inside."

Harriet reluctantly tucked her pipe back into the recesses of her field jacket.

"Both tenants seem to have disappeared, now, though," I said. "First her, then him."

"And they missed an appointment with a reporter," Emma added.

"Well, I can report that Ladd is alive in any event," Harriet said.

"He is?" I was suddenly wide-awake. "Where is he?"

"Guest of the state," Harriet said. "Safe and sound in the Mahina PD cell block."

"Jandie's husband was arrested?" Emma took the bottle and poured herself more whiskey. "Eh, Harriet, you kinda buried the lede there, ah?"

CHAPTER EIGHTEEN

"MOLLY, YOU WANT AN ICE PACK?" EMMA ASKED. I REALIZED I had my elbows on the table and was digging the heels of my hands into my eye sockets to push back against the throbbing.

"Yes please."

"She gets migraines when she's confused," I heard Emma explain to Harriet. "She gets 'em a lot lately."

"Stressed, not confused," I objected. "Okay, I'm also confused. Harriet, how do you know where Edward Ladd is, and why is he in jail? And most of all, why do I have no idea what's going on here?"

I felt like my eyeballs were about to pop out of my skull. Only the firm pressure I was applying with my hands was holding them in place, I was certain.

"I do a bit of pro bono work," Harriet said. "wonderful way to get to know where the bodies are buried. Not merely a figure of speech, it seems."

I felt Emma nudge the ice pack into my hand. I took it from her and planted my face in it. The cold immediately dialed the headache down from agonizing to merely uncomfortable.

"What happened?" Emma asked. "How'd they catch him?"

"They nicked him at the airport," Harriet said. "He had a one-way ticket to Honolulu."

"That's insane," I said. "He thought he was just going to hop on an airplane and somehow no one would notice?"

"Probably not thinking straight," Emma said.

"Well even if he's not as smart as he thinks he is," I said, "he has to be smarter than *that*."

I pressed the cold pack tight against my head, and took slow, deep breaths. With each exhale I visualized the pain seeping out of my eye sockets like used motor oil. It sounds gruesome, but it actually works.

"Edward Ladd wouldn't leave his precious aquarium," I said.

"Molly, he's a sociopath," Emma said. "He murdered his wife. You think he cares about some fish?"

"Brilliant," Harriet exclaimed. "So we're investigating then."

"What? No!" I pressed the cold pack into my forehead as hard as I could. "No, we are not investigating anything. The Mahina Police Department is on it, they've already made an arrest, and I know from bitter experience that they do not welcome help from well-meaning citizens."

"Oh, pish-posh," Harriet declared. "Rumor has it both of you been involved in a case or two."

Harriet herself had recently been accused of murder. Emma and I had been unavoidably pulled into the situation, but things had turned out well in the end. More or less.

"It was certainly an experience," I said. "Not one I care to repeat."

"We could just look into it a little," Emma said. "Molly, come on, don't you care about a murder happening on your own property?"

"You want to stick your oar in, you go ahead. Both of you.

Welcome to it. But I'm not inclined to sign up for anything like that again."

"I say, Barda," Harriet said, "do you know the story of the horse that wandered out of a village and could not be found?"

I set down the cold pack, which was no longer cold. Trying to understand where Harriet was going with this would just make my headache worse. I decided to nod along but be careful not to commit to anything.

"I don't believe I know the story, no."

"Well, the best minds of the village failed to locate the horse. But one day the village idiot walked into town, leading the missing animal by the bridle. When they asked him how he had done it, he said: 'Well, I just thought what I'd do if I was a horse, and then I went and did it.'"

"I see," I said, humoring her.

"I don't," Emma said.

"And neither do you, Barda. I'll give it another go. Now, what are we trying to do?"

"Prove Jandie Brand's husband killed her," Emma said.

"Let the police do their jobs," I said.

"You don't believe Jandie's husband killed her?" Emma shot back.

"It doesn't matter what I believe. The professionals, whose actual job this is, will figure it out."

"Barda, Nakamura," Harriet interrupted, "I'll thank you to call me Mr. Ladd for the next day or so."

"What?" Emma and I said at the same time.

"I will inhabit his mind. I will become him," Harriet said. "Rather Zen, don't you think so, Nakamura?"

"Ladd's mind is not someplace I'd want to inhabit," Emma said.

Harriet refilled her glass and drained it in two gulps.

"I am Edward Ladd. I am a formerly celebrated cartoonist fallen from fame, middle-aged and bald. My much-younger wife has surpassed me in every way. More famous, more beloved, and Heaven knows, far more attractive."

"If you wanna be realistic," Emma said, "no can talk all fancy li'dat. Ladd doesn't have an English accent. Oh yeah, and the real Edward Ladd tells everyone how smart he is every chance he gets."

"Well this is going to be interesting." I stood up. "Harriet, I mean 'Mr. Ladd', It's getting close to midnight and I certainly don't want to keep you."

Harriet stood up too.

"Say, looks like it's time to blow this joint and get some shut-eye." Harriet's nasal tone was apparently intended to evoke an American accent. "I'm gonna take a powder. Adios, amigos."

"I'd like Ladd better if he actually talked like that," Emma said when Harriet had gone.

"At least we have the rest of the week for her to get it out of her system before classes start again," I said. "Emma, I am so tired, I'm probably going to sleep late tomorrow. If you get up before I do, you and Pat can help yourselves to whatever you want for breakfast."

"Oh yeah, I know," Emma said.

CHAPTER NINETEEN

THE NEXT MORNING I WOKE UP AT SEVEN A.M., MUCH TO MY
annoyance. I hadn't slept well. The rain had been hammering
on the roof all night, and the power had gone out sometime
during the early morning. Pat and Emma were still asleep. I
dragged the portable generator out of the garage and plugged
the refrigerator in. I hoped I wouldn't have to throw any food
out. I went back into the garage to look for our long extension
cord, but just as I found it, the power came back on. When I
came back into the kitchen, the digital clocks on the stove and
the microwave were blinking and needed to be reset.

Emma popped her head up from the couch.

"Molly, you're up early. I slept good, you know." She
stretched her short arms over her head.

"I wish I could say the same."

"Eh, I forgot to tell you. You know those papers you were
worried your students were buying? I got a lead for you.
Check out OutsourceMyHomework dot com. That's the one
that everyone's…oh no, Molly."

Emma flung her blanket aside and hopped off the couch.

"Whoa, Molly, you look bad."

"Thank you?" I said.

"I know how it is. You get older, no can hold your liquor so good."

"It's not that, Emma, I just didn't get to sleep—"

"Eh, I got my sweatpants on already. I'll get us breakfast at 7-11. You like Spam musubi?"

"Yes please."

I wasn't on death's door; I was simply tired. Also, Emma had seen me before I had a chance to put on any makeup.

I wound up the power cord on the generator and dragged it back into the garage. By the time Emma got back I had made coffee for myself and was feeling better. Emma had a bag of Spam musubis, a 12-pack of Mehana Red Ale, and a copy of the *County Courier*.

"Check this out." Emma pushed the paper across the table to me. The headline above the fold read: *Social Media Star Disappears, Husband Detained.*

"Howdy Howell has the byline," I said. "I thought he was just doing upbeat human-interest stories."

"Things are a little different now with the husband in jail," Emma pointed out. "Eh, I know you got your problems with Harriet Holmes, but you gotta admit, she knows what she's talking about. She knew about Ladd going to jail before it was in the paper."

"Emma, I do not have a problem with Harriet. She's highly qualified and Mahina State is lucky to have someone of her caliber. Although I do have to ask, what kind of person gets sent to sexual harassment training and then makes improper advances toward one of the facilitators?"

"Maybe she took 'sexual harassment training' literally."

"Funny, Emma."

"It wasn't *unwelcome* improper advances, at least," Emma reminded me.

"Oh, I am aware. Now my headache's back. Ow."

"You stay right there, Molly. I'll get your ice pack."

Emma took the newspaper back and read to me while I

pressed the cold pack against my eyeballs. No one had seen Jandie leaving Mahina, according to Howdy Howell's story, and she was well-known enough to be recognized. She would have had trouble leaving town without anyone noticing.

The one ray of hope was the fact that no body had been discovered. Ladd hadn't posted bail, and he wasn't talking.

"Maybe he figures he's safer in custody," I said.

"Oh yeah, he's right about that," Emma replied. "Jandie's fans wanna dismember him."

Pat came over to join us at the table.

"You're a fan, Emma. So does that mean you want to dismember him?"

"Not if it means I gotta touch him. Ew."

"Good morning Pat," I said.

"Oh, no, Molly. Headache again? You want some hydrocodone?" he asked.

"No thank you. Makes me queasy."

"Eh, check this out." Emma handed Pat the copy of the *County Courier*.

"Walking around the airport with a one-way ticket?" Pat said. "That's funny. Almost like he wanted to get caught. Who is he protecting?"

"That guy, protecting someone?" Emma countered, "I think he's just a moron. Criminals aren't always masterminds, you know."

"It's almost lunchtime," Pat said. "Don't you guys have to be at work or something?"

"It's spring break," I said through the ice pack I had pressed to my face.

"Pat, you got somewhere to be?" Emma asked.

"Kind of. I'm meeting Howdy Howell for lunch."

"Tell him we all liked his reporting this morning," I said.

"Where are you meeting?" Emma asked.

"Not sure. We were gonna meet at the Pair-O-Dice, but I just found out the whole street's still closed off because of the flooding. We were gonna compare notes on the Jandie Brand disappearance. Not sure we wanna call it a case yet."

"Have him come here," I said. "I have a big pan of char siu fried rice in the freezer so as long as everyone's okay with that."

"You're okay with him coming here again?" Pat asked. "Last time you hid in your bedroom."

"If it makes things easier, Pat, I am happy to have you invite your colleague here."

"In other words," Emma said, "Molly's anti-socialness is defeated only by her nosiness."

"Okay, first of all, thank you for putting the most negative possible spin on my gracious offer of hospitality. Second, it's not 'nosy' to want to find out how my own tenant disappeared."

CHAPTER TWENTY

"GOSH, PROFESSOR BARDA, THIS IS AWFUL NICE OF YOU TO invite me to lunch." Howdy unfolded his napkin and tucked one corner into the top of his aloha shirt. I set the pan of fried rice down on the table and spooned a generous portion onto his plate.

"Howdy, do you think Jandie's husband had something to do with her disappearance? I'm not being *nosy*, I'd just like to know whether there's a murderer living on my property. Surely you can understand."

"I honestly don't know, Professor Barda, this was all so sudden. I never expected it. Although now that I think back… no, I better not say anything. In this country you're innocent until proven guilty."

He tucked into his fried rice, and I sat down, a little disappointed.

"For a smart guy, that attempted getaway was a dumb stunt," Pat said. "Ladd must've known he couldn't just try to fly out without someone noticing. Why didn't he go hide out in Kuewa, or stow away on a cargo ship?"

"So you think there might be someone else that might be involved, Pat?" I asked. "And Ladd is taking the fall for some reason? If someone else is involved, that means that even while Ladd's in jail, I could be in danger. At least Donnie and the baby are off-island but when they come back…is someone knocking at the door?"

It was Kaycee Kabua, our landscaper.

"Eh Kaycee, howzit!" Emma came up behind me, leaned out, and gave her a fist bump.

"I just left my sprayer in your carport on Sunday and I wanted to let you know I was getting it," she said.

"Hello there," said a voice behind me. "I'm Howdy."

Kaycee wasn't wearing her hoodie today. Her dark curls were loosely tied back, and her round face was prettily made-up. Howdy was so obviously impressed with her, he was practically wringing his hat (except he didn't have a hat) and tracing circles on the ground with his toe.

After I made introductions, Howdy offered to accompany Kaycee out to the carport to help her carry anything that needed carrying. Kaycee accepted his assistance, even though she didn't need it. She was easily capable of carrying the sprayer with one arm and Howdy with the other.

Howdy returned in an upbeat mood.

"Gee, what a terrific girl!" Howdy took his seat at the dining table and spooned a huge second helping of fried rice onto his plate.

"Right. Kaycee's great. So, where were we? Jandie Brand is in danger or possibly dead, her homicidal husband's in jail, we don't know who else is involved, our rental is a murder house, and I might be next."

Emma gave me a look.

"Am I wrong?"

"Aw don't be so pessimistic," Howdy said cheerfully "Know what they say, may as well look on the bright side. If things go bad, you can always cry later."

You can always cry later?

I turned to Howdy.

"You," I said. "Howdy, you were here with the Ladds. The day I dropped off the hurricane information sheet."

Howdy didn't deny it.

"Sure," he said. "It's possible. I've been over there a few times."

"What were you trying to talk Jandie into?" Emma asked.

"Talk her into? Why, nothing that I recall."

"Jandie said something about her landlady being a nosy crackpot," I said.

"Well I sure don't remember that particular conversation. But I can tell you where we had a little bit of, I don't want to call it a disagreement, let's say something that was under discussion. The *County Courier* expects its human-interest stories to have an uplifting tone. That's what I was shooting for. I hate to say it, but the way the couple was with each other, wasn't at all what I was hoping for. I was ready to write about a wife whose husband supported her fame and success. And a husband whose life was entering a second act, with his wife's support and a new generation of fans."

"So how come it wasn't what you were hoping?" Emma asked. "She hated him, I bet."

"I'm not sure it's right for me to go into too much detail," Howdy said.

"You must have been there that day," I said. "I heard two male voices in the house. Why would Jandie call me a crackpot?"

Howdy looked genuinely confused.

"I can honestly say, Professor Barda, that your name never came up."

"See?" Emma said to me.

"So what do you talk to them about when you go over there?" I asked.

Pat stood up.

"Don't mind me. I'm getting a cramp in my leg."

"Gosh, now that I think about it, I realize we always end up talking about Mr. Ladd's new book."

"He did say something about working on his writing," Emma said. "I thought that big *trombenik* was just saying it to sound important."

"Is there going to be a new book of cartoons?" I asked. "I'd be interested in reading it."

"Maybe it's a murder mystery where a husband does away with his younger and more successful wife," Emma suggested.

"No, it's neither of those things." Howdy pulled his satchel out from underneath his chair and produced a black, one-inch binder and a red-and-white flash drive. "I have a pre-publication copy right here. I didn't find much in here that I could use, but Mr. Flanagan, I thought you might be interested."

"Does Ladd know you have these?" Pat took the flash drive and binder from Howdy, handling them as gently as if they were baby birds.

"Oh sure, Mr. Flanagan, he's the one who gave them to me. He wouldn't mind you having them. He told me his publisher was having trouble lining up reviewers and if I knew anyone who was interested, I should share it with them."

"Is it about his life with Jandie?" Emma asked eagerly.

"No, she barely makes an appearance," Howdy said. "Missed opportunity, if you ask me. There's a lot of people out there who would buy anything having to do with Jandie Brand."

Howdy ran his hand through his hair.

"I know I shouldn't say this, but here goes. I think if you're married to someone, you should want them to succeed, and you should be proud of them when they do succeed. I think Mr. Ladd resented his wife's success. He thought he was the one who deserved to be famous, not her. I think he even thought she was standing in his way, if you can believe it."

Emma turned to me.

"You're a fan of this *putz*?"

"I did like his cartoons," I said. "Boy. That saying about never meeting your heroes is true, isn't it? Everything is disappointing."

"Oh, except this fried rice, Professor Barda," Howdy said brightly. "You're a great cook."

"I'll take credit for heating it up," I said, "but it's from Donnie's Drive-Inn."

"Can I keep this?" Pat asked.

"Oh, sure, Mr. Flanagan," Howdy said. "Like I said, I already read it. I'm no literary critic, but I gotta tell you, it's not something I'd put myself through again."

As soon as Howdy left, Pat inserted the flash drive into Emma's laptop. The three of us crowded together and read from the screen.

It was obvious why Howdy didn't want the book back. Ladd's memoir was an aggrieved, rambling screed, the main point of which seemed to be that the world seemed to be set up in a way that Edward Ladd found personally inconvenient. Ladd particularly seemed to resent the social pressure to treat as equals those he thought of as his inferiors. Which was just about everybody.

Pat stood up and walked over to the window.

"Don't mind me, I just need a break."

"Me too," I said. "I'm going to get something to drink."

"Bring the box," Emma called after me.

"If you plan to keep reading, you two should get on the liver transplant list now," Pat said. "From what I know of the guy, I don't think it's gonna get any better. Did you know he calls himself a certified master of persuasion?"

"I believe it," Emma said. "He musta been pretty freakin' persuasive to get Jandie to marry him. I'm thinking telekinetic."

"Here we go." I sat back down and placed the wine box on the table. "Have all you want. We can always buy more."

"Someone's at the door," Pat said. "I'll go get it."

It was detective Brian Medeiros. Pat invited him in, and we all moved to the living room. Detective Medeiros wouldn't have fit at the dining table.

"Is it true Edward Ladd was arrested last night?" I asked.

"That's correct," Medeiros replied. "I came by as a courtesy, to let you know he made bail. So don't be alarmed when he comes around."

"Did he tell you where Jandie is?" Emma asked.

Medeiros sighed.

"No."

"Great," I said.

"Look," Medeiros said. "Don't go out of your way to make contact him or anything like that, but if you see anything suspicious, you can call me. You have my card. Professor Barda, are your friends gonna stay with you?"

"Yes. You are, right?"

Pat and Emma nodded.

I nodded.

"Good," Medeiros said.

CHAPTER TWENTY-ONE

THE NEXT MORNING, THE STORY OF JANDIE BRAND GOING
missing had made it to the *County Courier* website. The
comments on the online article were as constructive and
enlightening as comments on the websites of local newspapers
usually are. I closed the browser window feeling dumber for
having read them. Enough internet for today, as the kids say.

The rain was hammering the metal roof, so I knew taking
a walk was out of the question. Pat was in the guest room and
Emma had gone to check on her house. I had already taken
care of all outstanding laundry, dishes, and bills. One of my
papers-in-progress had been revised and resubmitted and I
was waiting to hear back from the editor. My other paper was
currently with one of my coauthors.

For the first time in recent memory, my to-do list was
empty. I got up to fix myself a big pot of tea. I'd finally get
back to that murder mystery I'd been reading...

And then my computer beeped a notification. Another
draft business plan uploaded to the course website.

I sat back down at my computer. I'd realized long ago that
it was better to get grading done as assignments came in,
instead of letting them accumulate into a demoralizing pile.

The draft business plan was flawlessly formatted and clearly written. There was so little room for improvement, I couldn't even call it a draft. If this had been turned in as a final assignment, it would be an A paper.

The product described therein was a unisex undergarment equipped with a sort of replaceable filtration system. The executive summary led off with the product name and slogan:

Toot Sweet. Because your freedom ends where someone else's nose begins.

The company logo was an anthropomorphized can of baked beans, wearing a World War I-style gas mask.

It read exactly like the plans for "Party Pooper" and "Urine Luck." Structured as the assignment required, and free of spelling and grammar errors. There was no way these plans were written by three different people. And certainly not by the three different people whose names were on the assignments.

I noticed then that the rain had let up. I didn't have to deal with this right this minute, I thought. A walk would clear my head. I pulled on my shoes, grabbed an umbrella, and started walking uphill. The lush lawns and metal roofs gleamed from the recent downpour, and the air smelled electric. I went all the way to the cul-de-sac at the top of Uakoko Street, then turned around and went back down to the bottom. Feeling energized, I turned right and kept walking until I reached the lava rock marker at the entrance to the cemetery. The vast cemetery lawn was brightened with flower arrangements that families had left for their loved ones. I hadn't seen another person on the street, and I felt like I had Mahina all to myself. I inhaled deeply. The air was clean and fragrant. I wondered why I didn't go out walking more often.

And then the rain started to pelt down. I put up my umbrella, only to have a blast of wind immediately blow it inside-out, breaking two of the ribs.

I arrived home drenched and tossed the umbrella in the

garbage. I couldn't put it off anymore. I was dealing with an obvious case of academic dishonesty, and I was going to have to confront it.

Emma came back that evening with a big bag of avocados from her tree. Pat emerged from the guest room, and I set up a quiet dinner for three at the table. Pat told us he'd spent the day researching Tedd Ladd, but didn't find much other than that his old books of cartoons were abundant and cheap at online second-hand bookstores. He also mentioned that he'd tried to finish reading the manuscript Howdy had handed him.

"Any good dirt?" Emma asked.

"No. It's a completely self-indulgent sludge of Ladd's musings on life and on how awesome he is. It manages to be both boring and embarrassing."

"Maybe if he's that un-self-aware he'll let something slip," I said.

"You know, you're welcome to read the whole thing for yourself," Pat said.

"Not tempted at all," I said. "Emma, where did you go today?"

"There's that paddler party still going on at my house," Emma said. "I had to go check on the damage."

"I didn't know Jonah was into canoe paddling," I said.

"He's not. But him and the guys are all there partying right now. A couple of the paddlers from Kauai got their flights cancelled so they're stuck here."

"Kauai's getting hit hard right now," Pat said.

"Poor Kauai. Every time. Eh, Molly, you find anything out about those plagiarized assignments?"

"I think I got another one." I told Emma and Pat about Toot Sweet.

"These are actually good ideas," Emma said. "Toot Sweet, Party Pooper, what was the other one?"

"Urine Luck," I said. "I can't just ignore this."

"So then do the paperwork," Pat said. "Report them."

"Have you ever done the paperwork, Pat?" Emma asked.

"Not that I remember."

"Oh, you'd remember," I said. "The minute you upload a report, the Student Retention Office is all over your case. 'Can you prove the student knew he was supposed to turn in original work?' 'How can you be 100% sure that she didn't accidentally turn in the wrong document?' 'If you were a more caring teacher, your students wouldn't feel like they had to cheat.' They just keep making your life miserable hoping you'll give up."

"So don't do it," Pat said.

"Oh sure, sounds simple," Emma said. "Except if you let it go, you could get in trouble anyway. Remember that cheating scandal last year? Our administration was 'shocked, shocked' to find that plagiarism was going on. They blamed the faculty for not reporting when they should've. Eh, know what I realized? Our administration is exactly like army ants."

"They can skeletonize a cow in under two minutes?" Pat asked.

"They keep everyone walking around pointlessly in circles till they drop dead."

"Why do they do that?" I asked. "The ants, I mean."

"They're blind, so if they don't have any direction or leadership, they just follow the ant in front of them. Then more and more of 'em join in and pretty soon you got a big rotating disk of army ants walking themselves to death. It's kinda cool and disturbing at the same time. Look up ant mill if you wanna see it for yourself."

"That is interesting," I said. "Anyway, can we talk about my plagiarism issue now? I downloaded the three documents and checked the metadata. I didn't see anything suspicious. But then I noticed that one of the papers had the letters 'OMH LLC' in the footer. But only in the bibliography section."

"Did you look it up?" Pat asked.

"Yeah, I got almost a million results. An office cleaning company, financial services, grocery store, some little video game company. I don't know what it is."

"OMH is probably OutsourceMyHomework," Emma said.

"That's right," I said, "you did mention it before, didn't you?"

"That's the easy part," Emma said. "Now you gotta prove it."

"Speaking of proving things," Pat said, "what's Harriet up to? Is she still investigating your neighbors?"

"Oh yeah," Emma said, "she's getting inside Ladd's mind. Pretending to be him."

"Like method acting?" Pat asked.

"Yes," I said. "Including an American accent that seems to be payback for whatever Dick Van Dyke did in Mary Poppins."

"It sounds kinda nuts," Emma said, "but Harriet seems to know what's going on. Don't forget, she's the one who told us about Ladd getting arrested at the airport before the police did."

That night, despite the incessant drumming of rain on the metal roof, I managed to drop off to sleep. Only to wake up around midnight. Through the front window I saw the tawny glow of the sodium streetlight reflecting on the wet road. Everything seemed normal, and yet…I grabbed my phone, went out through the sliding doors onto the lanai and tiptoed around to the back of the house. From there I could see across the lawn to the rental unit. I watched it for a few minutes. At first it was dark and still, but then I saw light flickering inside, as if someone were creeping around with a flashlight.

I tapped on the window of the guest room to wake Pat, but he was sleeping soundly.

I remembered I had my phone with me and dialed the

Mahina Police Department non-emergency number. It rang and rang without going to voice mail. Then I called 9-1-1. The dispatcher picked up, but unfortunately, I'd connected with someone who was very serious about her responsibility to be frugal in her allocation of the county's resources. I was unable to convince her that a light in my rental unit constituted an emergency. She advised me to call back after 7:45 the next morning, when the non-emergency receptionist was on duty.

I marched back inside and found Emma was dozing on the living room couch. I shook her awake.

"Someone's in the rental," I said. "I can't wake Pat up. The police don't think it's important. I know this is a bad idea, but I think we should go take a look."

CHAPTER TWENTY-TWO

EMMA AND I TIPTOED ACROSS THE WET LAWN AND QUIETLY LET ourselves into the rental unit. We followed the sound of snoring to the master bedroom.

It was too dark at first to recognize the intruders. But when one of them stirred and the moonlight hit her face, I'm afraid I shrieked in surprise. The man next to her sat bolt upright, clawing at his sleep mask.

"Nigel!" I exclaimed. At the same time, Emma cried, "Harriet!"

"What on earth is going on?" I asked.

Harriet cleared her throat. "Say toots—"

"You don't have to do the accent," I interrupted her. "It's just us. Please tell me what's going on here."

"Right." Harriet groped at the night table for her glasses and slipped them on. "Ah, here we are. Oh I say, Barda, Nakamura, rather an inconvenient hour for a visit, what?"

"Harriet," I persisted, "Nigel, why are you two sleeping in my tenants' bed?"

Harriet removed her glasses, examined them, and put them on again. "Nigel didn't want to be left out of the investigation, you see, and I've already taken the role of

Edward Ladd. So Nigel's Jandie Brand, world-famous social media influencer and the center of our little drama."

"Hashtag-rather-a-cracking-good-adventure," Nigel said.

"Bit long for a hashtag, darling," Harriet said. "Did you sleep well?"

"Never better, my murderous little minx."

Nigel kissed Harriet's cheek, then jumped up and pulled on a flowered hapi coat that had been hanging on a bedpost.

"Fancy a cuppa, darling?" he asked Harriet.

"Is he wearing Jandie's robe?" I asked Harriet as Nigel sashayed out of the bedroom.

"He is," Harriet said. "Surely you don't want him running about in nothing but a pair of pink leggings."

"Listen, Harriet, I really do appreciate all the effort you and your husband put into this, and really, thank you for being concerned about my renters, but I wish you'd checked with me before you decided to stay the night here. What if Ladd had come back and found you two asleep here? I mean, we don't know what he's capable of."

"Fair point, Barda." Harriet threw aside the covers and started to pull on a pair of trousers over her long underwear. "I don't believe I'd have come to harm, not with Nigel here as protection. Still, I suppose one can't be too careful in lawless Mahina."

"Well, you've certainly committed to the Method, I'll give you that. Did you get any insights?"

"Oh yeah, you figure out what that psycho did with Jandie?" Emma asked.

Harriet frowned.

"The experiment was not a success, I'm afraid. Perhaps I'm too fond of Nigel. Committed as I was to the role of homicidal husband, I simply couldn't stomach the thought of doing away with him. Sounds a bit treacly when one says it out loud, but there it is. I say, is someone at the door?"

"I'll get it darling," we heard Nigel call.

Emma and I left Harriet to finish getting dressed and went out to the dining room. We found Nigel sitting at the Ladd's dining table having tea with Mr. Henriques, the next-door neighbor. The early morning sun slanted through the window, lighting up Nigel's colorful robe and snowy hair, and cruelly illuminating Mr. Henriques's bald head beneath his combed-over strands. I was so exhausted, it all felt like a dream. Although in retrospect the scene would have seemed surreal regardless of how well-rested I might have been. Unfortunately, this was my house, and it was up to me to take control of this mad tea party. I would have preferred to walk out and go straight back to bed.

"Mr. Henriques," I said, "what a surprise. What are you doing here?"

He jumped a little, sloshing his tea, then replaced his cup down carefully in the saucer.

"I was checking on Mr. Ladd's aquarium." Henriques said.

"How come?" Emma asked.

"I noticed activity inside the house, and I thought someone might be after the fish."

We all turned to look at the aquarium. The fish in question flicked back and forth serenely.

"Who would be after the fish?"

"Oh, no one in particular," Mr. Henriques explained. "But I promised Mr. Ladd I'd take care of his fish for him."

"How would you have gotten in if Nigel hadn't been here to answer the door?" I asked.

"Mr. Ladd gave me the key." Mr. Henriques beamed proudly.

I tried to remember whether there was anything in the rental contract forbidding the renters from sharing the key with someone else. Even if there were, what would be the point in enforcing it? Everyone would be mad at me and I'd probably get stuck taking care of the stupid fish myself.

"You did a good job, you, Mr. Henriques," Emma said. "The fish look happy."

"Yes, they're lovely," Nigel said. "Bit fiddly I understand, maintaining a saltwater aquarium."

"Oh yes," Mr. Henriques said eagerly. "It's a labor of love."

"Well I hate to be a buzzkill party pooper," I said, "but I'm going to ask everyone to clear out. Thank you for feeding the fish, Mr. Henriques."

"Want some coffee?" Emma asked as we re-entered my own house.

"No. Help yourself to whatever's there, though. Oh, I forgot you brought avocados. Hey, you can make avocado toast. Or guacamole."

"Nah, these are your avocados," Emma said. "Get plenty more at home."

"I'm too tired to eat right now. I'm going to try to get some sleep. Thanks for helping me clear everyone out and clean up."

"No worries. You're running low on cream though. I'll put a note on the refrigerator, so you don't forget."

CHAPTER TWENTY-THREE

THE NEXT DAY I SNEAKED REGULAR, NERVOUS PEEKS AT MY rental unit. Detective Medeiros had told me to expect Edward Ladd to return after he'd paid his bail. Ladd finally did come back that evening. I knew right away. Not because of my unceasing surveillance, but because he actually came by and knocked on my door. When I opened it and saw him standing there, I practically had a heart attack.

I was alone. Emma and Pat had left to do some grocery shopping and get takeout at Chang's Pizza Pagoda.

"No offense to Donnie's cooking," Emma had said. "But Chang's Pizza Pagoda got a two for one special on their cheesy kung pao shrimp pizza."

"I'll be moving back in, just wanted to let you know," Ladd said. "So you wouldn't think there was an intruder and call the police."

"Heh, call the police…that's a good one." I tried to force myself to smile. At that moment I would have been happy to refund the entire amount they'd paid for the lease, just to have Edward Ladd out of my life entirely.

Ladd stood on my porch, waiting. For me to ask him about

Jandie? For me to say I was glad to have him back? For me to invite him in?

"Can I...help with anything?" I asked.

"No, I just wondered what you thought of my manuscript."

Ladd knew we had his book? Were we supposed to have it, or was he trying to trick me into admitting I'd read it? What exactly had Howdy Howell told us? My brain helpfully reminded me that serial killers say the second murder is easier than the first, so I should be careful about what I say to Edward Ladd. *Thanks a lot, brain, now how about telling me exactly what I am supposed to say to this guy?*

"Your book?" I stalled cleverly, hoping the "master of persuasion" couldn't also read minds.

"I gave it to Howell," Ladd said. "He said he was going to give it to everyone he knows. That includes you."

"Oh, Howdy Howell. The reporter. I've only met him a couple of times, but I'll have to ask him about it next time I see him. A book, you say."

Misleading, but not an actual lie.

"If you want to assign it to your students, you don't need to ask permission," Ladd said. "Just make sure they're not buying bootleg copies."

"You have my word," I said. "I will never encourage my students to buy bootleg copies of your book. By the way, have you heard from Jandie? We're all really worried about her."

Ladd shook his head and without a word, turned and walked away.

Harriet came by that night about ten o'clock, with a big bottle of Irish whiskey. Before I could thank her, she told me it was a present for Pat.

"Why Pat?" I asked. "It's not his birthday or anything."

"It's Saint Patrick's Day," she said.

"Today's the eighteenth. St. Patrick's Day was yesterday."

"Was it? So easy to lose track during the spring holiday."

Harriet pulled out a chair and sat down at the dining room table. I joined her there.

"I know," I said. "I'm not really watching the calendar too closely either, but Pat and Emma went shopping today and came back from Mizuno Mart with a bunch of half-price marshmallow shamrocks and green candy corn."

"I see. I'm a day late. Can we call it Irish punctuality then? Where's yer man?"

"Pat's already asleep," I said. "It'd be like trying to wake the dead. Besides, he doesn't drink."

"Not really? Nakamura told me, but I thought she was taking the Mickey."

"No, it's true. Coffee's Pat's psychoactive of choice. But it would be a shame to let your generous gift go to waste."

"So it would." Harriet unboxed the whiskey. I went to the couch to shake Emma awake.

"So Ladd's back," Harriet said, once we were all at the table. "Any news about young Jandie?"

"So creepy, that guy," Emma said. "Doesn't even seem to bother him that his wife's missing. If I'd been here, I woulda said so to his face. I don't care, I'd take him on."

"It's probably better you were out then," I said. "I don't think you kicking him in the shins would advance the cause of justice. Also I appreciate all the food you guys brought home, so thanks."

"Eh, Harriet, this is how narcissistic he is. He asked Molly what she thought of his book."

"Ladd's got a book, has he?" Harriet raised her glass. "Any good?"

"No," Emma and I said at the same time.

"Any idea who the publisher is?"

"None," I said. "We just have the manuscript, not the final printed version."

"Hard to find a reliable publisher these days. Nigel's seems a bit dodgy. I'm not complaining, mind you, we're quids in, but their paperwork's a dog's breakfast. Filing our U.S. taxes is going to be an adventure."

"Speaking of money," Emma said, "it's weird that Ladd managed to make bail. Last I heard he was using the public defender and she was trying to argue the amount down cause he couldn't pay the original amount. I hope he hasn't gotten his murderer hands on Jandie's money."

"Ah, yes, funny that," Harriet said. "It seems a benevolent stranger paid his bail."

Emma and I turned to look at Harriet.

"Well he hadn't the money to pay it, had he? Here, go on." Harriet refilled our glasses.

"Seriously, Harriet?" Emma demanded. "*You* paid that psycho's bail?"

"Harriet," I said, "what are you going to do if he skips town this time? They already caught him trying to fly out of Mahina. If he leaves, you're going to be the one left holding the bag. I mean, you teach law, you obviously know this. I just...why?"

"He's not going to do anything useful while he's locked up," Harriet said cheerfully. "Far more instructive to observe the man in his natural habitat."

Emma opened her mouth to argue, but apparently changed her mind.

"Yeah, I see your point," she said.

"Emma, you what? This is insane. No. No one is observing anyone."

"Oh, and you say *I'm* bossy?" Emma retorted.

"I'm not bossing anyone. You two can do whatever you like. Just keep me out of it. I'm not involved in this at all."

"Plausible deniability, eh, Barda?" Harriet said.

"Yes," I said. "Sorry to be no fun, but I'm exhausted and I'm going to bed."

"Oh I say, you won't mind if I hang about tonight."

"What? Okay, why not. As long as no one does anything

that could get me sued or arrested, both of you, stay as long as you like. Help yourselves to anything in the pantry or the fridge. There's plenty of green candy corn. Harriet, thank you for the whiskey. It was delightful."

I thought Emma and Harriet would stay up for a while, drink some more, go to bed, and forget about everything by the next morning. I was wrong.

CHAPTER TWENTY-FOUR

I woke up the next morning to find Harriet Holmes still in my house. She was sitting upright in one of the armchairs in the living room wearing over-ear headphones and making notes in an old-fashioned notebook. Emma sat at the dining table sipping coffee and reading a paper copy of the *County Courier*. I started to say good morning, but Emma quickly put a finger to her lips. I made coffee as quietly as I could and brought my laptop over to the table.

"Man, make up your mind you baboozes," Emma muttered to her laptop.

"How long has Harriet been sitting there?" I whispered.

"She was there when I got up. Didn't want coffee or nothing. Eh Molly, can you help me with this?"

"Why are you filling that out now? We're not teaching this week."

"I know. It's from last week. I'm late. Again."

"Well. I should remind my faculty how lucky they are to have me fill those things out for them."

Emma lowered the laptop lid and stared at me.

"You're allowed to have your department chair fill them out?"

"Technically, no," I said. "But I fill these things out for my faculty anyway."

"How come?"

"Oh, let's see. Larry Schneider objects to everything the Student Retention Office does on principle and refuses to cooperate with them. Rodge Cowper has never met a deadline in his life. Hanson Harrison doesn't believe in email. And the first and last time Harriet Holmes uploaded her weekly classroom assessment, HR called me in and threatened to send my whole department to sensitivity training."

Emma lifted her eyebrows and turned to look at Harriet. Harriet was pressing her headphones to her ear with her left hand and scribbling furiously with her right.

"What'd she write?" Emma whispered.

"They wouldn't even tell me. So it's easier for me to just fill these things out myself. As long as I don't get caught. Please don't rat me out."

"Okay, what am I supposed to put on this line?" Emma turned her laptop around to show me the screen. "I never know what to write for this part."

"Ah. Here's what you do. Rephrase the question and then append the phrase, *by encouraging a growth mindset and honoring the students' individual learning styles.*"

"Seriously?" Emma asked.

"It hasn't failed me yet. So for this item your answer would be, *In BIO 101 I ensure understanding of the foundational course content by encouraging a growth mindset and honoring the students' individual learning styles.* For the next one, *I construct a safe and affirming learning environment in BIO 101 by encouraging a growth mindset and honoring the students' individual learning styles.*"

"No way. That's all I gotta do? I wish you'd told me sooner." Emma turned the computer back around and resumed typing.

"You're welcome."

"Oh yeah, thanks, ah?"

"Where's Pat?" I asked.

"He went for a walk."

I glanced out the front window. Sunlight glared off wet metal roofs across the street.

"I hope he took an umbrella," I said.

"Oh I say," Harriet blurted out, loudly enough to make Emma and me jump. "Ladd's got a visitor."

"Who is it?" Emma called back.

"Quiet," Harriet boomed. "I'm sussing it out now."

Emma stood up and pulled out her phone.

"I'll be right back."

Emma went into the kitchen, grabbed the bag of avocados, and walked past Harriet and out the front door. Harriet didn't seem to notice.

"It's a right knees-up now," Harriet said after about thirty seconds. "Someone else just arrived. A female. Don't think it's Jandie. Voice is pitched too low. She's saying something about avocados. Could be a secret code."

"Harriet, that's—"

Harriet held up a finger for silence and pressed it to her ear. Then she wrote something in her notebook.

The front door eased open and Emma came in quietly. She was empty-handed. I motioned her over to the table.

"You gave them my avocados?" I whispered.

"It was worth it," Emma said.

"So what happened?"

"Howdy Doody's over there with Ladd. They didn't invite me in, obviously, but at least I got to see who it was. Don't look at me like that, Molly. You weren't gonna eat half a dozen avocados by yourself in the next twelve hours, were you?"

"Did you leave me one, at least?"

"Yes, I left you two. I'm not a monster."

Harriet continued to listen and write. Emma worked on her weekly report. I read Donnie's latest email. Francesca seemed to be sprouting a new tooth, and Donnie's Uncle Brian had taught her to say "Vegas," which she pronounced "Bay-gus." Donnie didn't mention our renters, so perhaps the news of Jandie's disappearance hadn't reached him yet. Perhaps the whole thing would get resolved before Donnie had a chance to find out about it.

Through the window, out of the corner of my eye, I saw a Sampan drive by, heading down the street. It didn't stay in my field of view long enough for me to see the passengers.

"Well, that's sorted for now." Harriet lifted the giant headphones off her head, leaving her cropped gray-brown hair sticking out in all directions. "The sound quality's a bit of a disappointment. I didn't catch the names of the visitors."

"The man was Howdy Howell, the reporter," Emma said. "The woman was me. I brought over avocados to make 'em open the door so I could see who was there."

"Ah. Brilliant." Harriet scribbled more notes.

"What did you hear?" I asked.

"I thought you didn't wanna be involved," Emma said.

"Ladd and Howell were discussing the possible whereabouts of Ladd's wife," Harriet said. "Ladd's still claiming he doesn't know where Jandie is. Wouldn't be the first time someone's lied to a reporter for self-serving reasons."

"Did you find out *any* new information?" I asked.

Harriet stood and ran a hand through her hair. It looked exactly the same.

"No, not really. Something about Kuewa. It's where all the hippies and flower children live, isn't it?"

"And drug dealers, and people in witness protection," Emma said.

"They thought she might turn up there for some reason. She hasn't, of course. Rather a jolly wheeze listening in, though, makes one feel a proper spy. Can't wait to tell Nigel all about it."

CHAPTER TWENTY-FIVE

Harriet finally went home Friday afternoon. The following morning, Pat went out to spend the day at the library, and Emma settled in to finish up her Student Retention Office paperwork.

"Emma," I asked, "what was the name of that essay mill website again?"

"OutsourceMyHomework," she said, without looking up from her computer. "Dot com. Molly, they do custom-written assignments. You're never gonna find the evidence you need. You gotta give your students individual oral exams. Otherwise you're just gonna be playing whack-a-mole."

"Well, oral exams aren't in the syllabus." I brought over my own laptop to the dining table and set it up. "If I try to introduce them now, I'm going to get pushback and I'll get overruled by our administration in the end anyway."

"Yeah, that's true," Emma said. "Just plan 'em for next semester."

I started up my browser. The OutsourceMyHomework site had a welcoming layout and a cheery color scheme.

Welcome to outsourcemyhomework.com. We match up your order details with the most qualified writer in your field. We guarantee that your order is completed on time and to the highest standard. Find out how much your paper will cost.

I used the pulldown menu to select Business Plan, Undergraduate.

"Emma," I asked, "how much does your biology textbook cost?"

"I dunno. Couple, three hundred, I think. It's got a lot of color pictures though, that's why."

"So a custom-written business plan costs less than a biology textbook," I said.

"Yeah, but is it a thousand pages with color pictures?"

"Do you want to hear the customer reviews?" I asked.

"No."

"What about the ones from Hawaii?"

Emma looked up.

"There's reviews from Hawaii?"

"Yes! Listen to this. OutsourceMyHomework dot come is my go-to service whenever I need my homework done fast and quality," I read aloud. "They also do all kinds of unpopular subjects like arts, entrepreneurship, and pre-med."

"Sad." Emma went back to working on her computer.

"Here's another one," I said. "The speed of your writer are good. Your team is quick in replying and very helpful."

"I feel sorry for whoever ends up hiring that kid," Emma said.

"Aha!"

Emma looked up.

"Absolutely magnificent," I read. "I was very impressed by the speed and the quality of the assignment delivered. I could not imagine that homework services like outsourcemyhomework.com even exist. Finding this company is one of the best things that happened to me. For a reasonable price I got a business plan about a product called...Oh, for crying out loud."

"What?" Emma asked.

"I think I found our mysterious business plan writer. Emma, this must be for my class."

"So you gonna wait for someone to turn it in?" Emma asked. "And then bust 'em?"

"No, I'm going to give the cheater a chance to turn back. I'll send out a message to the class warning them against using essay mills. And I'm going to tell them if anyone is thinking of turning in a business plan for a product called 'Wee the People,' they should seriously reconsider."

"You're too nice," Emma said.

"Wow, that's not something I hear very often."

CHAPTER TWENTY-SIX

On Sunday morning, at what I can only describe as an unholy hour, my phone jangled me awake.

"I say Barda, have you seen the *County Courier* this morning?"

"Harriet?" I said. "The *County Courier*? Um, no, I haven't. What time is it—"

"I think you ought to check up on Ladd."

"Me? Harriet, what are you—"

But she had already hung up.

I went out to the living room, where Emma was snoring on the couch. I shook her awake.

"Molly, go back to bed," she mumbled. "What time is it anyway?"

"Harriet Holmes just called. She said I should check on Ladd. She didn't say why. I don't want to go over by myself."

"Make Pat go with you." Emma turned over and pulled the pillow over her head.

Pat and I found Ladd in bad shape. He answered the door wearing nothing but striped pajama bottoms. He was drinking from a coffee mug, but he reeked of sour booze. He was clutching the Sunday issue of the *County Courier*.

"You okay, man?" Pat asked.

"Uh, good morning," I said. How would I explain why we'd come by? "We just thought we'd check in."

"I guess you saw this." Ladd handed me the newspaper. The *County Courier's* top of the fold headline was *Body Found at Base of Cliff.* Pat leaned in to read over my shoulder.

A woman's body had been found at the bottom of seaside cliffs in the Kuewa district. The area was so inaccessible, the body had to be lifted out by helicopter. Her name was being withheld pending notification of her family, and anyone with information about the incident was asked to contact the police non-emergency line or Crime Stoppers.

"No, I hadn't seen this," I said.

"You think it's her?" Pat asked.

Ladd ran the heel of his hand up the side of his face.

"I hope it's not Jandie. But I haven't been able to reach her. Still. She doesn't answer her phone. She hasn't posted anything since she…for days now."

Ladd seemed genuinely distressed. If it was an act, it was a convincing one.

Or maybe his agony was real, only it wasn't over the Jandie's death. It was because he thought he'd hidden the body and it was only his bad luck it had been discovered.

Ladd didn't seem inclined to invite us in, and I had no particular desire to go into his sour-smelling house. I asked him to let me know if he needed anything. He (probably equally glad to end our interaction) assured me he would.

"Someone should keep an eye on that guy," I said once we were back inside my house. Emma was toasting bagels. The scent of seared starch was irresistible.

"Isn't that what we were just doing?" Pat asked.

"What happened over there?" Emma asked.

We told her about the newspaper story and how Ladd thought the dead woman might be Jandie.

"I think I know where that place is. Where they found

her." Emma came over to the counter and held out a plate with four buttered bagel halves. Pat and I each took one. "Paddlers stay away from there after a heavy rain, cause it's where all the *schmutz* comes pouring out into the ocean. Man, I hope the body they found isn't Jandie. How did Ladd seem? Suspicious?"

"He seemed pretty upset, actually," Pat said. Emma looked at me.

"He really did," I said.

"Oh, you don't believe me, but you believe Molly?" Pat objected.

"Maybe he was upset about the body being found," Emma said.

"That's what I thought too," I said.

"I'm gonna keep an eye on him." Emma grabbed a napkin, wiped her buttery fingers, and went to the front door.

"Where are you going?" Pat asked.

"To ask Harriet what she thinks. I bet she has some ideas."

"Oh, yes, let's get Harriet even more involved in this than she already is," I said to the closing front door.

"Jealous?" Pat got up and refilled his coffee cup.

"What? Jealous of Harriet Holmes?"

"You have to admit," he shouted over the noise of the coffee machine, "she's much better at this than we are."

I held off answering until Pat sat back down.

"Better at what, exactly?"

"She's creative. I hate the phrase, think outside the box, but that's what she does. She's not limited by—"

"Not limited by what? Tact? Manners? Decency? The rules everyone else has to abide by?"

"Whoa, Molly, did I hit a nerve?"

I sighed.

"Sorry, Pat. I didn't mean to snap at you. It's just that Harriet breezes around, doing whatever strikes her fancy at the moment, everybody loves her, and yet somehow she does things that always end up making more work for me."

"You're both independent adults, Molly. You're not responsible for her."

"Oh really? Tell that to HR. Did you know she told one of our marketing professors she'd been to his country and found it quite charming for a banana republic? Guess who got called into the principal's office? Not Harriet."

"I guess that's why they pay you the big bucks."

"What, to be a department chair? Ha, I wish. It's going to be interesting having Harriet living right up the street." I grabbed the last bagel half, which by now was room-temperature and a little leathery. "Okay, I still have time to get dressed and make it to Mass. By my calculations I'll get there just as they're finishing up the Passing of the Peace."

CHAPTER TWENTY-SEVEN

When I got back from Mass, Emma was lounging on the couch, playing a game on her phone.

"How was Mass?" she asked, without looking up. "You dodge the Passing of the Peace?"

"Mostly. What did you and Harriet get up to today?"

"I thought you didn't wanna know. Cause plausible deniability."

"I know, but I'm curious. Want a coffee?"

"Nah, I'm good."

I went to make a cup for myself and joined her in the living room.

"We tailed 'im," Emma said, almost causing me to spray my coffee.

"Ladd?"

"Uh-huh," she said.

"Emma, if he really is a murderer and he catches you following him, he's going to kill both of you, and I'll have to find someone to teach biz law in the middle of the semester. Unless he comes over and murders me afterwards, then it's not my problem anymore I guess."

"No worries. We kept outta sight."

"Is Pat here? He'd probably like to hear about this."

"I already told him the whole story. He's been holed up in his room. He says he has to file something before some deadline."

"He's not going to write about you spying on Edward Ladd, is he?"

Emma set down her phone on the floor and sat up.

"He better not, I said not to."

"So how are you so sure your target didn't see you?"

"Know what? That coffee smells good."

Emma came back with her own cup and sat on the couch.

"We used Harriet's da kine. The big headphones and that horn-looking thing you point in the direction you wanna listen. Works good, that thing."

"Is that legal?" I asked. "Never mind, she's a law professor. She would know. So what happened?"

"First, we hadda go into the cemetery right behind the rental unit to get a clear shot."

"So you and Harriet are standing in the cemetery, on a bright Sunday morning, wearing giant headphones and pointing the H.G. Wells ray gun at Ladd's house. Very low-key."

"You wanna hear about it or no?"

"Yes. Now I'm hungry though."

I opened the refrigerator and looked for the leftovers was sure I'd seen in there this morning.

"Hey, are you hungry?" I called from inside the fridge.

"Nah, I already ate your leftovers."

"Green candy corn it is." I poured some onto a paper towel and rejoined Emma in the living room.

"Anyway, we was taking turns, one of us with the headphones, the other one holding the umbrella. So when Harriet had the headphones on, she heard the front door opening and closing. So we decided to split up with me following him. I got in my car and caught up to him pretty quick cause he was walking."

"You followed a pedestrian in your car?"

"Yeah. I had to drive slow."

"He didn't notice a car driving next to him at three miles an hour?"

"Come on Molly, I know better than that. I drove behind him. An' the electric car's quiet. He didn't notice me. Anyway I followed him all the way down to Long's."

"Okay, and?"

"He bought some allergy medicine, a frozen burrito, and a bottle of Wild Turkey 101."

"Not exactly a smoking gun, Emma."

"Okay, get this. The cashier asked him for his birthday. So now I know his birthdate. It's cause of that law, yeah, they gotta card everyone who buys booze, even they're super old."

"Shoot, thanks for bursting my bubble. I always took it as a compliment when they carded me."

"Anyway Molly, I know what his birthday is now."

"Emma, I already know what his birthday is. It's on the rental application. Did he go anywhere else? Did he lead you to a body, or a cache of hidden murder weapons or something?"

"Honestly, I thought he was gonna. After he checked out, he took his paper bag an' walked all the way down to the hill to the ocean. He just stood there for a long time looking at the water."

"Oh. Then what happened?"

"After that he just walked back up the hill and went inside his house. So I came back here, and then you came in."

Pat came into the kitchen.

"Hey, ladies. Emma tell you about her gumshoe adventures?"

"Molly wasn't too impressed," Emma said.

"Hey, did you hear about my top-notch detecting?" I said.

"Actually, our top-notch detecting. Emma was the one who told me about OutsourceMyHomework dot com. I think that's where some of my students have been buying their business plans."

"I don't know why you bother," Pat said. "Why do you care more about academic integrity than your administration does?"

"You cared about it when you were teaching here," I said.

"At first, maybe," he said. "But I caught on pretty fast. I just started giving everyone A's as long as they turned something in. It made life easier for everyone."

"You *what?*" Emma exclaimed.

Pat ambled to the refrigerator and opened it. "I wasn't getting paid nearly enough to deal with all that B.S. with the Student Retention Office. You want me to work miracles? You're gonna have to pay more than minimum wage. You ladies hungry?"

I stood up.

"I am. I can heat up a tray of chicken katsu and teriyaki beef if I know I'm not the only one eating. Shoot, now what?"

I went to answer the door. Howdy Howell stood in the doorway, looking glum. I invited him in.

Howell plumped down on one end the couch and stared at his knees.

"I can't believe it. Jandie's gone. She's really gone."

Pat joined him on the couch. Emma and I quietly sat down at the dining table to give Pat and Howdy some space.

"Why do you think it's Jandie?" Pat asked.

"Who else could it be?"

A hearty pounding on the door made Howdy jump.

"I'll get it." Pat made his way to the front door in two long strides. "Oh, hey, Harriet."

Harriet Holmes swept into the room.

"Flanagan, brilliant to see you up and about. I say Howell, you look absolutely shattered. Yoo hoo, Nakamura, Barda, no, don't get up." She plopped down on the couch where Pat had been sitting. "You've all seen the news, I expect."

Pat took his displacement in stride and sat in a nearby chair.

"I can't believe Jandie's gone," Howdy repeated.

"Buck up, the body's not been identified yet." Harriet said encouragingly.

Howdy wiped the corner of his eye with his wrist.

"I hope you're right, Professor Holmes. But it sure is a coincidence, isn't it?"

"It's a wonder the body turned up at all." Harriet said. "It's rough seas down there. If it weren't for a daring 'opihi-picker, they'd never have found her."

"'Opihi-pickers are hard core," Emma said. "We lose one or two of 'em a year, just on this island."

"Really?" I said. "That's surprising. They're pretty experienced with the ocean, aren't they?"

"Even so. They fall off cliffs, or get trapped in rough surf," Emma said. "Just going by the numbers, 'opihi kill more people than sharks do."

"All that for limpets? Hardly seems worth all the fuss," Harriet said, "Manky little buggers. Taste like fishy rubbers to me."

"She means erasers," Pat said to Howdy. "Probably."

"What do we think?" Harriet said. "Misadventure, or murder?"

"It could have been an accident," I said. "Isn't it possible Jandie, assuming it is Jandie, was trying to get a photo and got too close to the edge of the cliff?"

Emma snorted.

"What are you thinking, Professor Nakamura?" Howdy asked.

"I think the husband did it."

"Wow. I sure don't like to think Mr. Ladd could have done something like this," Howdy said.

"You gotta think about it, Howdy," Emma said. "Even if you don't wanna admit it's possible. Reporters are supposed to be objective."

"I know." Howell looked dejected. "It's really hard. When I was interviewing them, I got to know them both pretty well. Jandie was a great girl. Down to earth, kind."

"Yeah, and the husband?" Emma said. "Egotistical pompous *schmuck* who probably killed his wife."

Howie shook his head.

"I never had any trouble with him, Professor Nakamura. Mr. Ladd could be real charming when he wanted."

"Just out of curiosity, Howdy." I said, "why do you call the husband Mr. Ladd but the wife Jandie?"

"I was raised never to call older people by their first names, Professor Barda. It's disrespectful."

Emma elbowed me. "Glad you asked?"

CHAPTER TWENTY-EIGHT

AND JUST LIKE THAT, IT WAS MONDAY AGAIN. SPRING BREAK
was supposed to have been a time to recharge, but now it was
over, I felt more frazzled than ever.

Maybe walking to work would burn off some stress. I left
my car in the garage and walked down Uakoko Street. It was
a good decision, I thought. The storm had blown over, and
the sky was shiny blue. I arrived at the old Territorial
Inebriates' Asylum building (where the College of Commerce
is now located) at seven-twenty and had the satisfaction of
being the first member of my department to arrive.

Retrofitting the old Territorial Inebriates' Asylum had
been no simple task. After several false starts, a black mold
scare, and an excavator malfunction that somehow shut down
the plumbing for several days, Konishi Construction had
finally gotten the climate control working. The only problem
now was that the air conditioning seemed to be permanently
stuck in the open position. I stepped into my freezing office
and opened the window a crack to let some warm air in.
Wasteful, I know, but my only other option was to sit there
getting blasted by frigid air until my sweat formed an ice shell
over my entire body.

Still feeling in a sunny mood from my walk, I settled down to deal with my in-box. My cheeriness ebbed as I went through the messages, starting from the most recent: A past-deadline assignment from Intro to Business Management. Then a few more. The campus newsletter. An announcement for a destination conference associated with an academic society I'd never heard of. A letter from one of my students complaining how unfair it was that she had worked so hard to get her assignment in on time only to have me postpone the due date at the last minute.

I stared at the email, baffled. I'd been so consumed with the issues in my Business Planning class over the break, I hadn't given much thought to the intro class. But I was certain I hadn't changed any deadlines on them. I used to hate it when my professors would change the syllabus around on a whim, and I was careful never to do the same to my own students. What was going on?

I found the solution to the mystery in the very next email, in the form of a campuswide announcement from the Student Retention Office, sent late Sunday night. The Student Retention Office welcomed everyone back from spring break with the announcement that "teachers" (by which the Student Retention Office meant the faculty) would accept late work without penalty because of the storm. And in case the "teachers" were uncooperative, the SRO helpfully provided a hotline for students to call and report them.

My phone rang. Harriet had come in to work and was calling from her office across the landing. She told me she had just seen the announcement from the Student Retention Office. It was utter bollocks, she informed me, and she had no intention of accepting any late assignments. But that wasn't what she was calling about, and could I drop by as soon as I possibly could? I got up, crossed the landing, and knocked on Harriet's door frame.

"Ah, there you are. Brilliant." She stood up. "The SRO

gets right on my wick. I've just changed my email settings. They're going straight into the spam folder from now on. Come along, we haven't much time. Nakamura's coming too."

"Coming where?"

"No time to waste, Barda. Off we go."

I locked up my office and followed Harriet down to the parking lot, where Emma was standing by her little electric car.

"Wanna drive, or walk up?" Emma asked us. "It's not that far."

"Not that far to where?" I asked.

"No time to walk." Harriet pulled open the passenger door and climbed into the back seat. I sat up front next to Emma. Emma drove uphill for two minutes and pulled into the parking lot of the Mahina Medical Center.

"There he is." Harriet pointed out Edward Ladd, who was walking into the side entrance. "Let's hang back a bit. We don't want to get too close."

"Why are we at the hospital?" I asked. No one answered me.

As soon as Ladd had gone inside, we got out of the car and went into the building through the same side entrance. Harriet pushed open an emergency exit door and led us down echo-y concrete fire escape stairs to the basement level. We emerged into a long, dimly-lit hallway, at the end of which was a grimy set of double doors. An ancient metal sign, black stamped lettering on pale yellow background, hung over the doors: MORGUE.

"Ladd's identifying his wife's body," Harriet whispered. She led us into a recessed doorway perpendicular to the morgue entrance and produced the listening gizmo from the folds of her field coat. "Can't be a fly on the wall, but this is the next best thing."

"Where were you hiding that?" I exclaimed. "And why am I here? I shouldn't be here. None of us should be he—"

"Shh!" Emma glared at me.

Harriet fiddled with some controls on the contraption and aimed it at the morgue doors. She produced a pair of headphones and set them on her head.

"Just the one pair, sorry," she said to us. "We can all listen after."

I could hear murmuring voices behind the doors, punctuated by the occasional scrape of metal. Judging by Harriet's shifting expressions, she was hearing a lot more than we were.

The doors swung open suddenly. The three of us backed up and ducked out of sight as Ladd walked out, with the much taller and wider Detective Medeiros right after him. We waited a few minutes to make sure the coast was clear, then retraced our steps back to the parking lot.

"Good to be back in the land of the living," Emma said when we stepped outside into the sunshine.

"I've never actually been down to the morgue," I said. "It is creepy. Even more than the College of Commerce building, and I'm pretty sure the College of Commerce building is actually haunted."

"Thought you'd like it," Harriet said.

We got back into Emma's car. Harriet took the front passenger seat this time, so squeezed into the cramped back seat. As Emma started back down the road, Harriet took out her listening gizmo, twiddled some dials, flipped some switches, and plugged a cable in to the dashboard of Emma's car.

"Showtime," Harriet said.

We heard a squeaking sound at first, like metal wheels. Then a quiet conversation. Men talking. At first it was hard to make out what they were saying. But I did recognize the voices of Edward Ladd and Detective Brian Medeiros.

Suddenly Ladd cried out. His voice was cut off, as if he'd clapped his hand over his mouth.

"Is this your wife?" Detective Medeiros asked gently.

"Yes, that's Jandie," Ladd said. "It's such a shame. She was so beautiful."

"Hard to look one's best in the circumstances," Harriet remarked.

"Weird," Emma said. "He doesn't sound too upset."

"Maybe it's closure," I said, "like it's better to know than to keep wondering what happened?"

"Ssh!" Emma waved her free hand at me.

"No water in the lungs," Medeiros was saying. "So she didn't drown. It's not official yet. Autopsy results haven't come in. But I thought you'd want to know."

"Oh dear," Harriet said cheerily. "She was found in the ocean, but she didn't drown. Murder with a body dump then."

CHAPTER TWENTY-NINE

EMMA AND I WERE SITTING AT THE DINING TABLE HAVING OUR morning coffee when we saw a police cruiser driving up the street.

We hopped up and ran through the kitchen, out to the lanai where we could get a good view of the rental unit. We watched two uniformed officers cross the lawn and approach the front door.

Ladd seemed to be expecting them. He followed the two officers right back out without any argument, carrying what looked like an overnight bag.

"Arrested, released, sees his dead wife at the morgue, arrested again," I said.

"Can they do that?" Emma asked. "Arrest him, let him go, arrest him again?"

"I guess they can," I said. "They just did."

Emma and I watched the police car make its way up the narrow street, do an 18-point turn at the dead end, and drive away.

"Wow, the guy can't catch a break," I said.

"He doesn't deserve a break, Molly."

"You're right, he doesn't. Come on, let's go back inside. I need another coffee. I bet you do, too."

"Eh Molly, you know what's weird?"

"He seemed completely unsurprised to be arrested again?"

"Exactly," Emma said. "I bet he doesn't mind getting arrested cause it's making him as famous as his wife."

When we got back inside, I headed to the kitchen to make coffee. Emma sat down at her laptop, which was already open on the dining table. She typed while I brewed.

"A-ha!" she cried.

"What is it?" I fixed up two coffees, brought them over, and sat in the chair next to her.

"Look at this," she turned the computer toward me. "Ladd's cartoon books are so old they're outta print. There's only secondhand copies available. Look what they're going for now."

"Wow, those are some premium prices. People are really paying that much? But Emma, these are all private sellers. Ladd doesn't get any of that money."

"It's not just the money, Molly. It's the fame. He killed her cause he wanted her fame for himself and now he's getting it."

"What, really? Okay, granted, he only cares about himself. Still, think about it. Would you kill your spouse to boost your used-book sales, if it meant there was a good chance you'd spend the rest of your life in prison? Come on, who would sign up for that deal?"

Emma snapped her laptop shut.

"Molly, you and me, we can't see into the soul of someone like that. Assuming he *has* a soul. Maybe it's worth it to him. You know what Pat always says, about pride and spite being the main things that motivate people?"

"That's such a bleak view of humanity. I would hate to think Pat's right about this."

"Yeah, that's your pride and spite talking. Eh, let's talk about this later. I gotta get to class."

That evening, Emma and I were having an early dinner and discussing the day's events when Howdy Howell stopped by.

"Say, Professor Barda," Howell said. "Is Mr. Flanagan here? We were supposed to meet up a little later, but I was in the neighborhood."

"He's taking a nap," I said. "Would you like to come in?"

"Eh Howdy," Emma called from the dining table, "we're having leftover green candy corn for dinner. Want some?"

"And wine," I said. "We were just talking about Edward Ladd getting arrested again. Did you know about it?"

Howdy hesitated, as if unsure how to answer.

"Come in, have a glass of wine," Emma said.

"Come on," I urged, "join us."

He hesitated and looked at his watch, and at me.

"Thanks, Professor Barda. I suppose I can throw a little fuel into the engine."

For appearance's sake I quickly assembled a plate of crackers and cheese and placed it in the center of the table. I got a glass and a small plate for Howdy.

"Oh, *now* you set out the good stuff," Emma said.

"Emma, if you wanted crackers and cheese, you could've said something. You can have whatever you want, you know that. So Howdy, how are you?"

Howdy paused and set down the cracker he was eating.

"I'm okay, Professor Barda. In fact, I'm better than okay. It looks like Jandie's finally going to get some justice."

"You wanted Ladd to get arrested?" Emma asked.

Howdy sighed.

"Not at first. It took me a while to come around to reality. But yeah, as disappointing as it is, you gotta face the truth. Kaycee thinks Ladd's guilty, too."

"Kaycee Kabua? Our landscaper?" I asked.

Howdy nodded.

"Sure, we're friends now. Good friends. Professor Barda, I can't thank you enough for introducing us—"

"You know what, you can just call me Molly," I said. "Only my students call me Professor Barda."

"Oh, I don't think so, Professor, thanks all the same. Pat told me I should call you Professor Barda and Professor Nakamura. Especially Professor Nakamura."

Emma narrowed her eyes. "*Especially* Professor Nakamura? How come?"

Howdy rubbed the back of his neck.

"Um, he just, I mean, he said it was what I should do."

"Pat gave you good advice, Howdy," I said. "It's always a good idea to use people's proper titles, but Emma's especially sensitive about being talked down to because of her h-e-i-g-h-t."

"You think I can't spell?" Emma pushed her chair back and stood up.

"What? Oh, shoot, sorry. I'm used to doing that around Francesca. Emma, I didn't—"

Emma made a rude hand gesture and stomped off toward the guest room.

"Pat!" she yelled. "What are you saying about me you bald-headed babooze?"

"I see what you mean," Howdy whispered to me. "She's kind of touchy, isn't she?"

"I heard that!" Emma bellowed from down the hallway. "I should come out there and knock that stupid straw hat right off your head."

"Emma, you're thinking of Mortimer Snerd," I called back.

"What?" Howdy said to me.

"What?" I said to Howdy. "I'm sorry, what were we talking about?"

Howdy brought a quaking glass up to his mouth, splashing wine all over his hand.

"I can't remember."

"Are you okay?"

"Yes ma'am, I mean, yes, Professor Barda. I'll just wait here for Mr. Flanagan. I expect his nap is pretty much over."

CHAPTER THIRTY

THE NEXT DAY NEWS OF EDWARD LADD'S ARREST WAS everywhere. Pat Flanagan and Howdy Howell had a double byline on the front page of the *County Courier*, but the story was big enough to go beyond Mahina. The Honolulu paper and the wire services had picked it up: Social media star missing, presumed dead. Husband arrested. Some of the longer stories would mention, a few paragraphs down, that Edward Ladd had at one time penned a popular cartoon under the pen name Tedd Ladd. But, the writer would add, Mr. Ladd had been out of the public eye for many years.

It was a struggle to keep class on track. My students already knew, of course, about my celebrity tenant. I was used to discouraging their efforts to pry.

"Jandie and her husband chose Mahina because we treat them like neighbors, not like novelties," I would explain. "Jandie already posts about where she goes on the island, what she buys, what she eats. We can always read her timeline if we want to know more about her. That should be enough to satisfy our curiosity. Otherwise, let's let them live their lives and be happy here."

But my usual deflections weren't enough to fend off the

questions I was getting today. How did he kill her? (We don't know for a fact Jandie's husband killed her, I told them.) Were there any signs they weren't getting along? (Not that I saw, but I hardly ever saw them because I tried to mind my own business.) After my tenant was murdered, was I scared for myself? (No, I told my students. This was a lie.)

I came home that evening emotionally exhausted, to find a pile of what looked like bills and junk mail on the dining table. Emma must have brought the mail in.

I poured myself a glass of wine and sat down to deal with the mail. A happy surprise was a postcard from Donnie, which had been sent from the airport in Las Vegas the first day they landed. A not so happy surprise was a letter-sized lime-green flyer folded in thirds. The return address was the Uakoko Street Homeowner's Association. Underneath my name and address was stamped, Unauthorized Rental Violation: First Warning.

This I did not need. My homeowner's association was hassling me now, over my respectively murdered and incarcerated tenants? I hadn't even known it was against the rules to have renters. Who can remember all the different things you sign when you buy a house?

I started to unfold the paper and noticed there was no postage stamp. That meant it hadn't been properly mailed; someone had just stuck it in my mailbox. I had heard only the Post Office was allowed to stick things in people's mailboxes. Was that still true?

A quick online search confirmed my hunch. I may have committed an infraction against the Uakoko Street Homeowner's Association, but whoever stuck this piece of paper into my mailbox appeared to have violated Federal law.

Too bad I don't know any lawyers who would be interested in this, I thought. Then I realized I might know one after all.

Petty, I know. But in my defense, I'm not the one who started it.

I phoned Harriet Holmes. She picked up right away and urged me to come by in person. By the time I'd made the short walk up the street she was standing in her open doorway, waving me in. Even from the sidewalk, I could smell pipe smoke.

I followed Harriet inside. Because her hands were full (pipe in one hand, and a glass of what looked like whiskey in the other) I closed the front door behind us.

"Oh, ah, hello." Nigel, Harriet's husband, was ensconced in the telephone nook with a small laptop open in front of him. His bushy white eyebrows drew together, prominent on his purplish-red face.

"You remember my department head, darling," Harriet said. "Molly Barda."

"Molly. Quite." The eyebrows relaxed. He ran a hand through his already-tousled white hair. "Yes, of course. Delightful. Delightful."

The last time I'd seen Nigel Holmes, he had been wearing Jandie's flowered hapi coat and pink leggings. The occasion was obviously more memorable for me than it had been for him.

"This is the first time I've seen your place since you moved in," I said. "It looks nice."

But Nigel had already tuned me out. He was staring at his computer screen, typing away.

"Don't mind him, Barda, he's rushing to meet a deadline." Harriet led me over to a rather impressive bar, set her glass down, and with her pipe clenched in her teeth, poured me what looked like a double shot of excellent whiskey. It would have been rude to refuse, of course.

"Let's leave him to it," she said. "It's lovely out on the lanai right now. Don't worry about the mosquitos. We've got it screened in."

"He's working on his, uh, prison memoir?" I asked as I followed Harriet outside. We got seated at a stylish teakwood table with matching (and surprisingly uncomfortable) chairs. Harriet set the whiskey bottle on the table. Next to it she placed a small wooden stand that turned out to be a resting place for her pipe.

"Mm. The publisher's an absolute tyrant about deadlines from what Nige says. But he doesn't seem to mind. Keeps his mind engaged, he says."

The sun sinking behind the mountains rendered the vast cemetery two-dimensional in the shadowless twilight. I decided I preferred the view from my own backyard. If I didn't feel like staring at a graveyard every time I went outside, I could just tell Kaycee to let the foliage grow up a little higher. But Harriet's house was further up Uakoko Street and at a higher elevation than mine. There was only the low retaining wall separating the backyard from the graveyard below.

"Harriet, thank you for having me over on such short notice." I produced the plastic bag that held the green folded flyer. I'd already touched it, but I didn't want to contaminate it more than necessary. "This was left in my mailbox. It's not actual mail. It's a crime to tamper with the U.S. mail, isn't it?"

"Ah yes? May I?"

Harriet opened the bag and pulled out the paper.

"Oh, I was trying to avoid fingerprints—"

"This sort of paper doesn't hold fingerprints well," she unfolded the paper and smoothed it on the table. "And nobody's going to test for fingerprints in any event. It's a few hundred dollars' fine at most. No prison time, if that's what you're hoping for."

"Of course not." Prison for putting a flyer in someone's mailbox did sound a little excessive when she said it out loud.

"Ah yes, our ever-vigilant homeowner's association. Hmm, nuisance, vacate immediately, daily fine, oh, it's all here, isn't it? No, she can't do any of it."

Harriet folded the paper and handed it back to me.

"She?" I asked.

"Head of the homeowner's association. Asked me for legal argle-bargle she could use to sort out a resident who was running an illegal rental. Had no idea it was you she was after, Barda. Terribly sorry."

I gazed out at the dark cemetery and sighed.

"I did not realize renting was against the rules. I mean, I know we read through the CC&Rs when we bought the house, but I had about a thousand papers I had to sign and initial. I'm starting to wish we'd never build that rental in the first place. Harriet, what can I do?"

"Ignore it."

"Really? Sounds like kind of a daring legal strategy."

"Linda likes to make herself feel important," Harriet said, "but when it comes down to it, she can't do any real harm."

"Are you sure? Because…wait a minute. Did you say Linda? Likes to feel important? As in wielding what little actual authority she has in the most obstructive, bureaucratic, and misery-making way possible?"

Harriet took a deep pull on her pipe and blew a stream of smoke into the night air.

"Sounds like you know her."

"I think I may. Is her last name Wilson by any chance?"

"Indeed. Linda Wilson. Ah yes, of course. Recently retired from the Mahina State University Student Retention Office."

CHAPTER THIRTY-ONE

H̲arriet refilled my glass up to the top. I did not
object. Not only was the whiskey excellent, but the teak slats
of Harriet's stylish outdoor chair were cutting into my
backside. Harriet was wearing her heavy field coat. She
probably had no idea how uncomfortable her furniture was.

But worse by far than my physical discomfort was the
prospect of Linda Wilson, my nemesis from the Student
Retention Office, in charge of my homeowners' association.

"Dangit. I had no idea she lived on my street, much less
that she was the head of the homeowners' association. I even
chipped in for her retirement gift. She's never going to stop
persecuting me about this rental, is she?"

"I wouldn't worry. Know what I think? She's put out that
she never was able to meet Jandie Brand. Feels snubbed. But
she can't admit it to herself, so instead she bangs on about
peace and quiet and the unique character of our beloved
Uakoko Street. Once this murder business is over it won't be a
problem."

"Why? What's to dissuade her from what is apparently her
lifelong mission to make my life miserable? And now she's
retired, she can spend all day harassing me, can't she?"

"Well, she's not exactly got the moral high ground here. She's renting to Nigel and me, after all."

"Linda Wilson is your landlady?"

Harriet nodded and released another plume of pipe smoke into the night air.

"Wow. A few weeks ago I didn't even know Linda Wilson even lived around here," I said. "I thought I'd never have to think about her again after she retired. Now I find out she's in charge of the whole place."

"She's harmless, really." Harriet set her pipe down and refilled our glasses with her excellent whiskey. "Now, I've got a question for you. Our missing girl, Jandie Brand. Always dressed to the nines, was my impression."

"Mine too. Whenever I saw her, she was always put together. Trendy clothes, fancy eyebrows, the whole thing. I think I remember her telling me designers sent her clothes and makeup for free. Hoping for the exposure. She never had to go clothes-shopping if she didn't want to."

"I thought as much. Barda, would it surprise you to learn that when she was found, she was dressed in drab and definitely unfashionable clothes? Like one would find at the Oxfam."

"The what? Oh, Oxfam. Second-hand clothes. Here it would be Goodwill or Salvation Army. Sorry, that's not really important. Yeah, it's not like Jandie to wear thrift store stuff, but if she wanted a disguise…wait a minute. Harriet, how do you know what Jandie was wearing when she died? We didn't see the body."

"Never mind about that. My point is, there's a theory the poor girl may not be Jandie Brand after all. If she isn't Jandie, two interesting questions arise. Who is she? And where is Jandie?"

"Well now, hang on. If I were Jandie, trying to escape from my abusive husband, I would do something out of character to throw him off."

"Fair point. Sad to think she went to all the effort for nothing. It's something to think on."

It had gotten completely dark while we were talking. The cemetery was now a sea of shadow, studded with moonlit gravestones. I took my leave and headed home. It was a good thing I had come on foot. Harriet was a generous hostess, and her whiskey was, as I may have already mentioned, excellent.

When I came back in, the house smelled comfortingly of pizza and coffee. Pat and Emma were at the dining table.

"Where've you been?" Emma demanded as I poured myself a glass of water and joined them. The Chang's Pizza Pagoda box lay open in the middle of the table, containing a few slices of veggie pizza. I told them about my conversation with Harriet.

"Linda Wilson lives right here on your street?" Emma exclaimed. "No way. And she's in charge of the homeowners' association?"

"I thought it was just bad luck we ran into her that one time," I said. "Nope. She was patrolling her territory."

"No way. Molly, you gotta move."

"Emma, I'm not going to let Linda Wilson chase Donnie and me out of our own home."

"How's Nigel's prison memoir going?" Pat asked.

"He was working on it when I went over there. According to Harriet, his publisher is keeping him to some strict deadlines."

"Maybe," Pat said.

"What do you mean maybe?" Emma reached for another slice of pizza.

"I don't know. Maybe Harriet is exaggerating to make Nigel's work seem more important and sought-after than it really is. This whole thing with Ladd got me thinking. People will pull some pretty outlandish stunts to promote their books. Remember when Emma started a riot at that speakers' event on campus?"

The accusation caught Emma mid-bite.

"Not," she protested through a mouthful of pizza.

"You kind of did, Emma," I said. "So Pat, you don't think Nigel Holmes' gritty tale of minimum-security prison is the blockbuster Harriet says it is?"

"Has she told you the dollar amount of the advance, or is it all just 'loads of dosh' or whatever?"

"It would be weird if she went around telling people the exact amount, Pat."

"He's been going over Ladd's manuscript, that's why," Emma said.

"Oh, brave man." I slid a slice of pizza onto my plate. Bamboo shoots and bean sprouts aren't my favorite pizza toppings, but I hadn't had anything solid for dinner. "I couldn't get past the first couple of pages. Are there any clues in it about Jandie's murder?"

"I thought you couldn't make money by writing a book about your crimes," Emma said.

"Son of Sam Laws," Pat added. "Although, those only say you can't profit from writing about the actual crime. And even with that narrow interpretation, they haven't always held up in court. That's not really relevant here anyway. There's practically nothing in there about Jandie. He says something once about how other guys are jealous of him cause his wife is young and hot."

"Here he is married to one of the biggest celebrities in the world," Emma said, "and somehow he thinks people would rather read about him."

"Do you think he was having an affair?" I asked.

"Only with himself, as far as I can tell," Pat said.

"Hey, that reminds me, Molly," Emma said. "Remember that Post-It you found in the house?"

"You know, I forgot about that." I pulled up the photo on my phone. "Here it is. It's hard to read the writing, and the picture quality's not great. Do you think it means anything? As far as this case?"

Emma leaned in to look.

"You shoulda focused better and held still. It's kinda blurry. I bet you moved, that's why."

"At least I remembered to take a picture of it. This looks like a number. Hornet? C-o-s-h. A cosh is something you hit someone with." I said.

"Yeah, that doesn't mean anything to me," Emma said.

We cleared off the pizza box and paper towels. Pat went to bed, Emma took her usual place on the couch, and I settled in to read Edward Ladd's manuscript on my computer. To the extent there was a plot, it was this: Edward Ladd was an "intimidatingly intelligent" and bookish child, who, we are told, bested bullies with his wit (although the specifics were absent). As a college student he chafed at "useless" breadth requirements and "stultifying" classes. He eventually dropped out of college, vowing never again to Let Schooling Interfere With his Education. Edward Ladd, in his telling, was the smartest guy in the room, the hero of every story.

"Find any clues yet?" Emma called over from the couch.

"Pat was right," I said. "No murder here. Unless you count him boring the reader to death. The only good thing about it is it's mercifully short. What are you doing?"

"Looking through Jandie's posts," Emma said.

"That sounds way more interesting. Find any clues? A sinister figure lurking in the background of one of her photos?"

"Nah. It's just her in different places around the island." Emma flipped through the posts. "There's a lot of cooking and recipes. Farmer's market. Hey, here she is at Donnie's Drive-Inn."

"I remember that. It was nice of Jandie to feature the Drive-Inn. Donnie told me we had a little bump in business after her posts."

"Here she is at the Bayfront. Hey, that's our canoe halau in the background. Ooh, sketchy boardwalk, must be Kuewa. She actually makes it look good in the picture though. Here's a plate with dragon fruit and a cut-open papaya. Jandie eating loco moco pizza rolls—"

"Chang's Pizza Pagoda?" I asked.

"Yup. Ooh, here's hot malasadas. Man, this is making me hungry."

I plunked down on the chair next to Emma's couch.

"I don't know why we're doing this," I said. "The police are on it. The mayor is even interested. What do we know that they don't?"

"We know Jandie personally, Molly."

"Did you ever actually meet her?"

"We can't just ignore her murder, pretend like nothing happened and everything's fine. Besides, the mayor doesn't care about Jandie. He just doesn't want any bad publicity getting out about Mahina."

"I guess so."

Emma sat up and gave me a friendly punch in the upper arm.

"That's the spirit, Molly!"

"Well, I've looked through Ladd's manuscript," I said, "and I haven't found anything resembling a clue."

"Yeah, I've gone through Jandie's timeline like ten times. Nothing out of place. She's posting like normal, then it just stops."

"So now what?" I asked.

We sat quietly for a moment. Emma brightened, and shoved me excitedly.

"Molly! Call the number!"

"Great idea. What number would that be?" I rubbed my upper arm.

"The number on the Post-It we found. That you took a picture of."

I pulled my phone out and found the picture. I showed it to Emma.

"This one?"

"That picture's junk. I can't tell whether those are ones or sevens," Emma said.

"Me either. And that could be a 4 or a 9."

"We can read the rest, so that's three digits with two possibilities each," Emma said. "Two to the third is eight possibilities. So we only gotta try at most eight phone numbers."

"So on the seven-eighths chance it's not the right number, what do you say when someone picks up?"

"I get them to identify themselves then say sorry, wrong number."

"And on the one-eighth chance it's not a wrong number, you might be making contact with an actual murderer. Know what? If this were a movie, right now I'd be screaming 'just call the police, you ding-dongs' at the screen. So how about tomorrow I call Detective Medeiros and share your brilliant idea with him?"

CHAPTER THIRTY-TWO

THE FIRST THING I DID THE FOLLOWING MORNING WAS CALL the Mahina PD non-emergency line. Emma made us coffee while I spoke with Detective Medeiros.

To my surprise, Medeiros had actually followed up on the Post-It note I'd found.

"That phone number is Little Jack Horner's," Medeiros told me. "It's a bakery down in Kuewa."

"Oh yeah, I've heard of it. It's supposed to be good. That's why the note said *Horn*," I said.

"Yes. We already investigated the area. No sign of Jandie Brand."

"What about cosh? Why was that about?"

"Not sure."

I hung up. Emma was watching me.

"So?" She handed me a cup of coffee, already sweetened and doused with cream.

"The phone number is Little Jack Horner's," I said.

"Oh yeah, the café in Kuewa. Jandie did a photoshoot from there like a month ago."

"Makes sense. Darn it, what was I thinking, a murder clue on a sticky note would be right there in the house for me to find? And of course the police have already checked it out. It's their actual job."

"Let's go there anyway," Emma said.

"Why? Do you think there's something the police might have overlooked?"

Emma held up her phone, displaying a photo of a smiling Jandie Brand, sitting at an outdoor table, brandishing a pair of chopsticks at what looked like an entire cheesecake in front of her. The caption was stuffed with hashtags:

#lilikoi #pie #passionfruitpie #Hawaii #Hawaiilife #cakevspie #sweet #jungle #beautifulhawaii #tropicaldreams #islandlife #Jandistas

"Jack Horner's got the famous lilikoi chiffon pie," Emma said. "I always wanted to try it. You no get class today, ah? We could go now."

"All the way down to Kuewa? It's a long way to drive for pie," I said. "But you're right, I'm not teaching today, and I don't have to be in until later. Are you sure?"

"I got a progress report due tomorrow and it's due noon East Coast time. Which means I really gotta submit it today. And I am teaching class this afternoon. But if we start now, we can get back in time."

I took our coffee cups to the sink.

"Just to be clear," I said, "we are not interfering in a police investigation. We're just going to Kuewa for pie."

"Oh yeah, hundred percent," Emma agreed.

Little Jack Horner's was about forty minutes out of Mahina. The narrow, intermittently-paved road was crowded on both sides by strawberry guava bushes and staghorn fern, and canopied with Albizia trees. Emma almost drove past the hand-painted sign marking the location of Little Jack Horner's. Tacked on to the main sign was a cardboard placard announcing "Fresh" Eggs Today!!

Emma slammed on the brakes, backed up, and steered into

a gap in the foliage. I was thankful we hadn't taken my car. Having my 1959 Thunderbird scraped up by wayward strawberry guava branches would have broken my heart. At the end of a long gravel driveway was a dirt lot with around half a dozen parked cars. Two of them were late-model Mustang convertibles, obviously rentals. The bakery itself was a tin-roofed plantation-style house with a wraparound lanai. A few patrons were eating and taking selfies at the outdoor tables.

Emma pulled over to the side of the gravel lot and parked. We stepped out into the hazy sunshine.

"I can smell the coffee from here," Emma said. "Man, I'm hungry."

"This place must be pretty good for people to come all the way out here on a weekday morning," I said. "Hey, thanks for driving."

"Yeah, good thing we didn't bring your car, Molly. I don't think it woulda fit up the driveway."

"I was thinking the same thing," I said.

Directly inside the bakery building was a counter where we were to place our orders. A woman in her forties seemed to be in charge. She was a of a certain Kuewa type: leathery tan, sun-bleached strawberry blond hair, wrist tattoo that had blurred over time. She wore a dark-green apron tied over a blue-and-green batik dress.

"You still get eggs for sale?" Emma asked, when we had reached the front of the line.

"Sure do. How many dozen you want?"

"Just one dozen," Emma said.

"A dozen for me too," I added.

"Rainbow!" the woman barked. The woman called Rainbow appeared from somewhere in the back. She looked to be about the same age and general type as her boss, but the years had been harder on her. "Two dozen eggs for these ladies please."

"Two dozen eggs," Rainbow repeated to herself, and went back the way she'd come in.

"Do you have lilikoi pie?" I asked.

"Our lilikoi chiffon pie? Only one piece left."

Emma and I looked at each other.

"She can have it," we said at the same time.

"Eh, look at us," Emma said, "All like da kine, Solomon."

"We can split it," I said.

"She's paying," Emma added. "What? I drove."

"That's fair."

"We make our lilikoi chiffon pie fresh every day," the woman said. "You should check in next time you're in the neighborhood. Now, you can't make a breakfast out of half a piece of pie. How about our omelet aux fines herbes? It's our specialty. Eggs are from our own happy hens."

"I don't think I'm hungry enough for an omelet," I said. "Just pie and coffee for me, please."

"I like try one omelet," Emma said.

There were no other customers lined up behind us, so we got to chatting while our food was being prepared. Our chatelaine 's name was Phoenix. This was not her birth name, obviously, and in fact she wasn't the first "Phoenix" I'd met here. Phoenix is a common name among people who have moved to the island to reinvent themselves. Sometimes after escaping a bad marriage or quitting a tedious job. Often after enrolling in witness protection.

"Were you here when Jandie Brand did her photoshoot?" Emma asked.

"Who?" Phoenix lifted the lone pie slice out of the display case.

"Little hapa girl, straight black hair, high voice?" Emma said. "She's a social media influencer."

"We get a few of those. They buy one or two things and take up a table for two hours while they take pictures of their food." Phoenix handed me a tray with two skinny slices of pie (she'd pre-split it for us) and two coffees. "Rainbow will bring out your omelet. Be patient. She's new."

"Oh. Is she from…next door?" Emma asked.

Phoenix turned to Emma.

"Be kind. That's all I'm gonna say. We can all use a little kindness."

Emma and I found a table out on the lanai. We were surrounded by jungle. It was warm but not too hot, and the coffee smelled delightful.

"What's 'next door'?" I asked as soon as we sat down.

"It's a rehab place for women. Not one of the fancy kind. More like a halfway house."

"How do you know so much about it?" I asked. "You've been here before?"

"Yeah. With the paddlers. We were checking out the sewage situation."

I paused mid-sip and slowly set my coffee cup down.

"No worries, Molly, their water supply's fine."

"Are you sure?"

"Yeah, it's just the wastewater. Their heart's in the right place, you know, trying to help these women out. But they get more people staying there than they're supposed to. So their cesspool's overloaded and the stuff leaks out and ends up in the ocean. All these rains we had haven't helped, you know. The paddlers were trying to raise money to help them close the cesspool and get a septic tank instead. Costs a lot more than you'd think, and there's the maintenance too."

"What's the difference between a cesspool and a septic tank?" I asked. "I thought they were the same thing."

"A septic tank is enclosed and has to be pumped out every so often," Emma said. "A cesspool is just a hole in the ground lined with rocks. Eventually the stuff leaks out. Yeah, you should wrinkle your nose Molly, it's gross."

"Just letting sewage ooze out into the groundwater? How is that allowed?"

"Lotta places down here in Kuewa are on cesspool. Somehow people trust it to act like some frickin' enchanted well that magically sanitizes everything. Newsflash, it doesn't work like that."

"Well. I just learned something. Now I'm going to try to stop thinking about cesspools and enjoy my tiny piece of pie. Mm, it is good. Emma, how many people do you think know there's a halfway house next door? If you hadn't said anything, I would never have suspected."

"They keep a low profile. No sign outside, and they let the trees grow up an' hide the building."

The woman called Rainbow brought out our eggs. She plunked the mismatched cartons on our table and left without saying a word. I opened the cartons to make sure the eggs weren't cracked. They were intact, and smaller than store-bought eggs and varied in color: white, brown, and blue-green. They also needed to be washed.

"Hey look," Emma showed me her phone. "Jack Horner's has vacation rentals."

I looked at the online listing.

"I bet they don't have a homeowner's association hassling *them*. Where do people stay though?"

"Probably over there." Emma pointed to a cluster of tiny houses on the far side of the property, just visible behind a screen of trees.

"Those look exactly like the emergency shelters from the last lava eruption," I said.

"Maybe they are," Emma said.

"I've always been curious about those little houses. What do you think they're like to stay in?"

"Why, you gonna set some up on your property? Like some kinda super slumlord?"

"No, I was thinking when Donnie comes back it might be fun to spend a night down here. Francesca would enjoy seeing the chickens too."

Emma and I stopped by the counter again on our way out to buy some creampuffs we'd seen in the display case.

As Emma started to back out of the parking spot, something occurred to me.

"Emma, that place next door. It's a women's shelter?"

"More like a halfway house, but yeah, pretty much."

"Is it possible Jandie's there? Hiding out from her husband? Maybe she planned her escape when she did the photoshoot."

"How do you explain the body they found then?" Emma countered. "Her husband said it was her."

"Maybe he's bluffing," I said. "Maybe he misidentified the body on purpose."

"What for?"

"So the police will stop looking for her and leave him free to track her down? I don't know."

"How's he gonna look for her if he's in jail? I know, Molly. It would be awesome if Jandie was still alive. But I don't think she is."

I couldn't argue with that. Emma guided her car back down the narrow driveway. The only sound was the scraping of branches against the car doors.

"You know the Cloudforest isn't far from here," I said. "Do you want to stop and say hi to Mercedes Yamashiro before we go back? I don't know, maybe we don't have time."

"I'm about to go on the highway. Right or left? Pick one. You gotta be more decisive, Molly."

"Right."

"I know I'm right."

"I mean turn right. I don't get down to the Cloudforest that often. Also, might as well check how things are going with our interns.

CHAPTER THIRTY-THREE

I HAD STAYED AT THE CLOUDFOREST BED AND BREAKFAST
when I first arrived in Mahina. Mercedes Yamashiro, the
proprietor, had taken me under her wing. She'd even tried to
introduce me to Donnie.

I wasn't interested. At the time I was dating the Stephen
Park, the theater professor. Stephen had turned out to be
faithless, self-absorbed, and a terrible human being all around.
I should have listened to Mercedes and not dismissed Donnie
the "plate lunch salesman" out of hand.

Emma drove hard over a pothole, which broke my chain
of thought.

"So anyway," Emma was saying, "I told 'em, yeah, fine, it's
supposably legal now, but it doesn't mean you can use my
house as a...Molly, are you listening?"

"Of course. You're telling me a story about...your
brother?"

Safe guess.

"Jonah can be such a pain in the *tochas*," Emma said.
"How does a grown man end up being such a useless waste of
carbon?"

"Didn't you try to fix me up with him?"

"I never," she said.

"You set up a meeting at Sprezzatura," I said. "You, me, and Jonah. At the fanciest restaurant in Mahina. And then you backed out at the last minute, hoping that with just your brother and me there, it would magically turn into a date."

"Yeah, so?" Emma demanded. "What's wrong with Jonah? I still think you two woulda made a good couple."

Emma's little brother Jonah is undeniably good-looking, but notoriously scatterbrained.

"Emma, *you're* the one who told me he's 'dumber than an empty box of stupid'."

"He is. And you're smart. So if you had kids, it'd balance out. Eh, you gotta admit, my brother's a better catch than Stephen Park. What a *putz* he was. Glad you dumped him."

"Can't disagree with you there."

"Shame, ah? Bad representation for Koreans."

"What are you talking about? Stephen wasn't Korean."

"Half Korean then."

"No. Emma, we talked about this. Park is a Scottish name. Stephen Park was zero percent Korean."

"But then how come—"

"Stephen let everyone think he was half-Korean because in his mind being hapa was cooler than being some plain old white guy whose wealthy parents subsidized his theater career with the profits from their Beverly Hills-Adjacent plastic surgery center."

"Oh wait," Emma said. "I think I remember something about that."

"Don't you remember how Stephen used to sneer at me for abandoning my literary education? How 'degrading' he thought it was for me to be working in the, gasp, horrors, *business school*? And here he was, a bigger phony than I could ever *dream* of being."

"Wow, Molly, sounds like you're still mad at him."

"What? Of course I'm not," I said. "That would be petty."

"You should be mad at him. Remember when he lost track of time and missed your birthday cause he was *schtupping* his theater student?"

"Oh, *that* part you remember. Hey, here we are. I didn't realize the Cloudforest was so close."

"Time flies when you're trashing your ex." Emma steered into a parking spot.

The young woman at the desk was one of the College of Commerce interns. I knew her from Intro to Business Management class the previous year, so we got to chatting about her internship. She told me she liked Mercedes and enjoyed most of the guests, and she was learning to deal with the occasional difficult customer. Mercedes wasn't there, so I left a message. Emma bought a jar of guava butter from the display behind the counter.

"Oh, tell Professor Harriet I hope her thumbs feel better soon," the young woman said as we turned to leave. I turned back.

"Professor Harriet Holmes?" I asked.

"Yeah, Professor Harriet is great. I'm taking her business law class this semester. I always heard b- law was boring but Professor Harriet makes it super interesting."

"I'm happy to hear it," I said.

"She get all these stories about high maka maka British guys she knows, like politicians and archbishops and stuff. Did you know what a 'rent boy' is?"

"What happened to Professor Harriett's thumbs?" I asked. "Why did you say you hope they feel better?"

"Oh our class did pretty bad on our last midterm. Someone asked her aren't you supposed to make sure we all pass? And she told us the grades would stand but she expected the Student Retention office would have her in thumbscrews for it."

"I think it was just a figure of speech," I said. "The Student Retention Office doesn't have actual thumbscrews."

"Really?" Relief washed over the young intern's face.

"It *is* the Student Retention Office though," Emma said. "You never really know what they're capable of."

CHAPTER THIRTY-FOUR

WE GOT BACK TO MY HOUSE AROUND LUNCHTIME AND FOUND
Pat sitting at my dining table, working on his computer and
drinking coffee. I set out the box of cream puffs and we sat
down to catch him up.

"And look at these." I opened the carton of eggs to show
him. "Authentically farm fresh, complete with dirt."

"So they don't need to go in the fridge," Emma said.

"Wait, really?" I said.

"Yeah, really. Don't look at me like that, Molly."

"Yeah, according to my mom they never refrigerated their
eggs back in the old country," Pat said.

"Okay. I guess I won't put them in the fridge then. Pat,
anything interesting happen while we were gone?"

"Someone named Kaycee called," Pat said. "Is she the one
who does your yard?"

"There is a Kaycee who does our yard," I said. "Thanks,
I'll call her back."

"She said don't call her. She wants you to call Howdy
Howell."

"Why should we call Howdy?" Emma asked. "Isn't he
your friend, Pat? You call him."

"No one asked *me* to call him." Pat went back to whatever he was doing on his computer.

"That doesn't sound right," I said.

"Here's Howdy's number if you want to call it." Pat held out a sticky note.

"Guess we're calling Howdy." Emma plucked the paper out of Pat's hand.

"Ow!" Pat shook his hand. "Paper cut!"

Emma dialed the number on her phone. I was happy to let her deal with it. I tidied up in the kitchen and tried to make as little noise as possible.

"Hey Howdy, it's Emma Nakamura. Kaycee called. Yeah. Uh huh. Eh, why don't you just come over here and help us figure out what's going on."

"What is going on?" I asked when Emma had disconnected the call.

"He didn't want to talk about it on the phone. Pat, do you know what's this about?"

Pat stopped typing and looked up from his computer. "No. I hope he's okay, though. I don't think he's ever done a real crime story before."

"What, you think it's gonna mess him up or something?" Emma asked.

Pat shrugged. "It can take a toll on you."

A few minutes later, Howdy Howell stood on my front porch, looking disoriented.

"I can't believe it." He wandered into my living room, looking around as if it were his first time there. "I just can't believe it."

"Come in," I said. "Sit down. We have coffee and cream puffs."

"Thanks so much, Professor Barda. Professor Nakamura."

Howdy sat at the dining table. Pat pushed the pink Jack Horner's pastry box over to him. Howdy flinched.

"Sorry, Mr. Flanagan," he said. "I can't think about eating right now."

"You gonna be okay?" Pat closed his computer and set it under his chair.

Howdy shook his head.

"I'm not worried about myself, Mr. Flanagan."

I set a fresh cup of coffee down in front of Howdy. He accepted it gratefully.

"What on earth is going on with Kaycee?" I took the last empty seat at the table. "Why did she tell us to call you?"

Howie sipped his coffee and set it down.

"Wow, thanks, Professor Barda. Kaycee's in jail."

"Kaycee?" I exclaimed.

"For what?" Emma asked.

"For murder," Howdy said.

"Nah, nah, nah. I can't believe Kaycee would murder someone," Emma said. "It's not like her at all. And believe me, I don't say that about all my students. Who did she murder, supposably?"

"Jandie Brand," Howdy said.

"Kaycee loved Jandie Brand," I said. "What possible reason would she have to hurt her?"

"Doesn't necessarily let her off the hook," Pat said. "Remember 'fan' is short for 'fanatic.'"

"So what's her bail?" Emma pulled out her phone, presumably to check her bank balance. "I can chip in. I know she won't skip town."

"They're holding her without bail," Howdy said. "Professor Barda, Kaycee said you could help because she works for you and she was your student at Mahina State."

"She was Emma's student, not mine," I said. "But she does do yardwork for Donnie and me."

"She's hoping you can convince them she's not a flight risk," Howdy said.

"I mean I'll tell them she's a great landscaper and a reliable worker," I said. "I can't say I know her that well."

"I'll vouch for her," Emma said. "What is wrong with people?"

"What about Ladd?" Pat asked. "Is he off the hook?"

Howdy shook his head.

"I think the theory is they planned it together. Kayce Kabua and Edward Ladd. So they could be together, I guess."

"Wait," I said. "They think Kaycee was having an affair with *Ladd*? What on earth is her motivation?"

"Ladd's rich and famous," Pat said.

"He's not *that* famous," Emma said. "I mean, no one recognized him at Long's."

"And we ran their credit report before they moved in," I added. "They're comfortable, but I wouldn't call them rich. I mean, if they were rich, they'd be staying at one of the resorts, wouldn't they? Not renting a single-wall plantation house next to a cemetery in Mahina."

"People can surprise you," Pat said. "I mean, if I had a nickel for every time I've thought, ew, no way are *those* two having an affair, I'd have a disturbingly large amount of nickels."

"I really like Kaycee," Howdy said. "She's a great girl. And I came here because she asked me to ask you for help, and I said I would. But…I mean, I'm not an expert. Who am I to think I know better than a judge?"

"So you want us to try change the judge's mind or no?" Emma demanded.

Howdy shook his head. "I don't know, Professor Nakamura. Poor Kaycee. Maybe she's safer where she is? It's all so confusing."

"What evidence do they have against Kaycee?" I asked Howdy.

"I don't know, Professor Barda."

"Does she have a lawyer?" Emma asked. "Honey Akiona's the best, if you want my advice. Expensive, though."

"I don't have a lot of savings," Howdy said. "But I'll pitch in what I can."

"I wanna go talk to her," Emma said. "Molly, you come with me. Pat and Howdy, you go do your investigative reporting thing."

"But—" Pat started.

"What, you got something better to do?"

"Yeah, okay. Whadda you say, Howdy," Pat said. "Should we try to make ourselves useful?"

CHAPTER THIRTY-FIVE

IT WAS QUICKER TO GET A PHONE CALL WITH KAYCEE AT THE Mahina police cellblock than to schedule an in-person visit, so Emma and I dialed in the next morning. Kaycee sounded surprisingly cheerful as she filled us in on her situation.

An anonymous tipster had directed police to Kaycee's carport, where they had retrieved a shovel with traces of blood on it.

Kaycee told us she had no idea who might have called in the tip, or how her shovel had gotten blood on it. She was always careful to clean up after a job, she said. She would never put away a bloody shovel with her other tools. When Emma told her about the theory that she'd been having an affair with Jandie's husband, Kaycee laughed out loud. Why would she want to get with some grumpy old fut like him? She liked Jandie Brand and would never want to harm her, who would be dumb enough to think she would? Kaycee told us jail wasn't so bad. One of the guards was a friend from high school. So were a couple of the inmates.

Kaycee didn't seem to grasp the fact she was in real trouble. She seemed to think it was all a big mistake that would get cleared up quickly.

"What do you think?" I asked Emma when we'd hung up. "Is Kaycee lying about not having an affair with Ladd and covering for him? He killed Jandie, and she's taking the blame?"

"Who was the snitch?" Emma asked. "That's what I'd like to know. Who called the police and told 'em about the shovel? Who would wanna pin this on her?"

"I don't know. Maybe she slighted someone and didn't realize it, and they're getting back at her?"

"That's a heck of a way to get back at someone," Emma said.

Pat came into the kitchen, rubbing his face, and set up a cup of coffee for himself.

"Morning, sleeping beauty," Emma called into the kitchen.

"Late night?" I asked.

"Yeah, but worth it." Pat brought his coffee out to the table and joined us.

"So we have a cause of death." Pat sipped his coffee. "For Jandie Brand."

"For the mystery corpse we *assume* is Jandie Brand," I said. "Although the only person casting doubt on her identity is Ladd, so it's probably her."

"Oh, I know," Emma said. "Beaten to death. With the bloody shovel they found in Kaycee's garage."

"Wrong," Pat said.

"Drowned?" I suggested. "Someone pushed over the cliff into the ocean?"

"Wrong again."

"I give up," I said.

"Not me," Emma said. "Wait. Okay, I give up too."

"Overdose," Pat said. "There are significant injuries, but they're postmortem."

"I would not have guessed an overdose," I said. "Is it

wrong for me to be relieved to hear it? I mean, that she wasn't alive to suffer?"

"I kinda agree," Emma said.

"Did you get to talk to Kaycee yet?" Pat asked.

"We just finished," I said.

"Did Kaycee tell you why she had a bloody shovel in her garage?"

"She had no idea how it got there," Emma said.

"Carport, not garage," I said. "So someone could have planted a bloody shovel there. Or smeared blood on one she already owned. We were wondering who would've called in the tip."

"Ladd?" Emma suggested.

"But he's in jail too, isn't he?" I said. "Can you call in an anonymous tip from jail?"

"You can snitch in jail," Pat said. "It's kind of a tradition, in fact."

"Implicating Kaycee wouldn't clear Ladd anyway," I said. "It would just support the theory that the two of them were having an affair and conspired to get rid of his wife."

"Except Ladd could say Kaycee was obsessed with him and killed his wife so she could have him to herself and he's the real victim," Emma said.

I stood up and headed to the kitchen.

"Ugh. I need a drink, but it's only nine-thirty in the morning so that drink's going to have to be coffee. Also I'm hungry now, which is weird."

"Maybe someone really, really wanted Jandie dead," Pat was saying when I came back with my coffee and a plate of reheated wontons and chicken katsu. "Overdosed her, beat her with a shovel, then threw her into the ocean. Real belt-and-suspenders approach."

"How much of this is public?" I asked Pat.

"They're not releasing her cause of death," Pat said.

"They want to keep the murderer in the dark. So don't you two say anything."

Howdy Howell stopped by the house later that afternoon. He thanked Emma and me for calling Kaycee and told us she really appreciated our reaching out to her. He and Pat went out to the lanai to talk privately. I didn't mean to eavesdrop, but the warm breeze carried the men's voices through the open window.

"Mr. Flanagan, I'm telling you this in strictest confidence," Howdy Howell said. I should have stopped listening then and there, but humans can't exactly seal off their ears, can they? "I liked the Ladds a lot, and I always thought Mr. Ladd was a decent man, but now...Kaycee is telling me the shovel they found isn't hers. She says someone planted it at her place. Does that make any sense to you, Mr. Flanagan?"

I glanced over at Emma. She was relaxing on the couch and reading one of her plant biology journals. Maybe she couldn't hear the conversation going on outside.

"So who are you thinking it was?" Pat asked.

"I hate to make an accusation," Howell said quietly. "He was always real decent to me."

"But?" Pat prompted him.

The wind must have changed direction. Either that, or Pat and Howdy started talking more quietly.

"Dang it." Emma sat up.

"Emma, were you eavesdropping?"

"Oh yeah, like you weren't." Emma came over and pulled a chair up next to my desk. "We gotta find out what Howdy told Pat. I bet he was talking about Ladd. How are we gonna get Pat to spill, that's the question."

"I wish I could stay and help," I said. "But I have a homeowners' association meeting in about an hour."

"Ugh, really? Since when is your stupid HOA more important than squeezing the truth out of Pat?"

"Since I learned our nemesis Linda Wilson was in charge

of it," I said. "I need to be prepared for whatever knavery she's planning to inflict on me next."

"Yeah, okay. You get a pass."

"Want to come?" I asked Emma. "They're having it at Harriet and Nigel's place."

"No way. If I die without ever laying eyes on Linda Wilson again, I'll consider it a life well lived."

CHAPTER THIRTY-SIX

THE FRONT DOOR OF THE NEW HOLMES RESIDENCE WAS AJAR. I let myself in and placed the heated-up tinfoil tray of chicken katsu on their kitchen counter with the other potluck dishes. When Donnie had brought home the foil trays from the Drive-Inn and packed them into the freezer, I thought it was way too much food for the short time he'd be out of town. I was wrong. The frozen food stash was coming in handy.

I found the standing-room-only crowd out back, packed into the screened lanai overlooking the cemetery.

Presiding over the meeting was my erstwhile nemesis from the Student Retention Office, Linda Wilson. Even though it was a warm evening, Linda wore one of her signature long-sleeved muumuus. She passed out meeting agendas printed on lime-green paper. The meeting itself was routine—treasurer's report, modest increase in annual dues—until the last item.

Vacation rentals.

"We all moved here to Uakoko Street because it was such a *peaceful* neighborhood," Linda announced, making eye contact with me for the first time that evening. "Although I haven't been able to determine any specific rules or covenants which have been broken with regard to rentals…" (and how disappointing for *you*, I thought) "…I think recent events will serve as a warning to all of us to screen our tenants carefully. On that note, let us thank *my* tenants, Nigel and Harriet Holmes, for the use of their house this evening."

"Hullo," Harriet called from somewhere in the back.

"Delighted," her husband Nigel added.

When the meeting was over the crowd moved inside to enjoy the potluck offerings. Harriet came over and clapped a hand on my shoulder.

"I say Barda, things do seem a bit tense between you and old Linda."

"It's completely unfair," I said. "Harriet, you know me. I'm not brave enough to fight the Student Retention Office. I always cooperated with them. Emma was Linda's real nemesis. Linda's problem with me was just guilt by association." There was a little more to it than that, but Harriet didn't need to know everything.

"Our gentle little Emma Nakamura? Never. However did it all start?"

I glanced across the room. Linda was far enough away to be out of earshot. Still, to be safe, I motioned Harriet outside. We stood next to the retaining wall separating the Holmes's backyard from the cemetery below.

"It all began back when the Student Retention Office had a campaign to go after classes with high failure rates. BIO 101, Emma's class, popped up on their radar. Linda Wilson went after Emma, trying to arm-twist her into giving more generous grades. According to Linda, Emma was crushing the dreams of future doctors and nurses. When Emma wouldn't cave, Linda went straight to Emma's dean."

I looked around to make sure no one was eavesdropping. Most of the guests had gone inside, and a few lingered on the lanai, drinking and chatting.

"So now Emma's dean is all upset about getting in the crosshairs of the Student Retention Office. He goes to Emma and tells her she has to fix things with Linda, but of course without lowering standards in BIO 101. Now Emma was in an impossible position. So she wrote out the whole story and published it to the campuswide listserv. She wrapped up by saying she would quit before she took advice on teaching biology from someone who didn't know Gregor Mendel from Josef Mengele. I don't know whether Linda got the reference, but she knew she was being insulted. She retaliated by referring Emma to Faculty Development."

"Ah yes." Harriet lifted her whiskey glass. "The Student Retention Office struggle sessions."

"Emma calls it de-education camp, because you come out dumber than when you went in. Anyway, I'm sorry you've have to deal with that, Harriet. Not the friendliest welcome to Mahina State."

"De-education camp, that's brilliant. Actually, I don't mind it. Rather a jolly wheeze, if you must know. One spends the day in a palatial sort of conference room with working air con, loads of snacks, and shockingly decent coffee. And if we're lucky, we get a little speech from Victor Santiago from alumni and community whatsis."

"Yeah, Victor Santiago kind of scares me too. Have you noticed he never smiles?"

"Victor scares you? I think he's dead sexy. I mean to say, I'm a happily-married woman, but what's the word? *Caliente.*"

"Okay. Listen, Harriet, it was really nice of you and Nigel to open up your house for this meeting. It made me feel a little less like I was entering enemy territory. Where is Nigel? I thought I heard him earlier."

"Back at his desk, I expect, working on his manuscript," Harriet said. "He's fallen a bit behind schedule, it seems."

I felt a cramp in the back of my leg and propped my foot up on the retaining wall. A stone dislodged and tumbled down to the cemetery below.

"Oh no, sorry about that." I took my foot back down.

"Harriet, speaking of Linda, you might want to ask her to get this retaining wall looked at. I'm not a structural engineer or anything, but I don't think retaining walls are supposed to have pieces falling off them."

"I jolly well will ask her to fix it. I've become rather attached to this place and I'd rather it didn't slide into the graveyard. I say, speaking of Linda, I'd heard she was having it off with one of our lecturers, and you and Emma found them out. I'd assumed it was why she disliked you."

"Emma and I didn't set out to expose her," I said. "We had no idea. We were looking into something completely different. But once you start turning over rocks…"

"Ah yes. No telling what sort of slimy abominations will come wriggling out. Oh I say, Henriques, you're a quiet one. You gave me quite a start."

Mr. Henriques, my next-door neighbor, had materialized next to us. In the moonlight, his big round moon head looked more moon-like than ever. He reeked of sour booze.

"Good evening Professor Holmes. Professor Barda. How are you on this fine evening? Or *is* it a fine evening?" Mr. Henriques's voice cracked. "Poor Jandie. Poor, poor girl."

Out of one of the multitudinous pockets of her field coat, Harriet produced a crisply folded handkerchief and handed it to Mr. Henriques. He blew into it with a loud honk.

"He didn't deserve her," Henriques sniffled. "Shame we don't have the death penalty in Hawaii."

"You think the husband's guilty then," Harriet said.

"I'm not talking about the age difference." Henriques tucked Harriet's handkerchief into his back pocket. "Nothing wrong with a girl wanting to be with a mature man. When's the last time he brought her flowers, you think?"

"I expect you know the answer." Harriet seated herself on the crumbling retaining wall, dislodging another stone. Mr. Henriques and I sat on either side of her. The stone was cold and damp, but there was no other place to sit.

Henriques pulled out his phone and showed us one of Jandie's photo posts, from about a month earlier. It showed a pretty but inexpensive coffee-can flower arrangement of waxy red anthuriums, torch ginger, ferns, and ti leaf, the kind you might buy at the Farmers' Market for ten dollars.

"Nice composition," I said.

"I sent the flowers. Me." Henriques pocketed the phone. "Anonymously. I didn't want credit. I just wanted to make her happy. The husband, all he cares about is his aquarium. He deserves to get the needle, that's what I think."

Having made his point, Henriques stood and made his unsteady way inside, heading in the general direction of the potluck dishes.

"Well, that was unexpected," I said.

"Was it really?" Harriet countered.

"I guess not. He's always struck me as a little odd. Linda!"

Linda Wilson materialized in a cloud of gardenia perfume and stale cigarette smoke.

"Hello Harriet. Molly. How nice of you to show up to one of our little association gatherings. I hope you didn't find it too boring."

"Never boring, Wilson," Harriet said. "I say, where are little Whatsis and Thingummy?"

"Pele and Hiiaka get stressed around crowds," Linda said. "Bob's watching them at home."

"Is that what they're called?" Harriet exclaimed. "Wilson, you named your dogs after two revered Hawaiian goddesses? Careful, that's the sort of thing that'll get you packed off to sensitivity training."

"I love the potluck idea," I interrupted. "And I always enjoy seeing people's houses and getting decorating ideas. I'm really glad I came tonight."

"Well, I must see to the other guests." Harriet stood. "Snacks and bevvies inside, whenever you're ready."

I watched helplessly as Harriet disappeared into the house, leaving me alone with Linda Wilson.

"Such a shame about Jandie Brand," Linda said. "I hope this doesn't ruin the image of our neighborhood."

"It's terrible," I said. "Everything that's happened. Poor Jandie."

"Yes. We should all try to be careful about screening our renters. I know I am. Well, you're new at this. You'll learn, I hope."

"You're absolutely right, Linda. I am new at this." I tried to figure out what Linda's game was here. Linda would have jumped at the chance to have Jandie Brand as her own tenant. But now things had gone pear-shaped, as Harriet might say. I figured there were now two possibilities. Linda was either:

(a) gloating at my misfortune, cured of her celebrity fever, and relieved Jandie's murder hadn't happened on her watch, or

(b) gloating at my misfortune, and convinced things would have turned out differently if only *she* had been the one renting to Jandie Brand and Edward Ladd.

"How did you get Jandie interested in your place to begin with?" Linda asked.

Ah, so the answer was (b).

"I actually asked Kaycee to help us advertise the place, I said. "I'm not sure exactly which listing brought them in. She's good at social media. She uses it to publicize her landscaping business."

"But after they saw your house up close, they still agreed to rent it?"

"Yes, they did," I said. "It's brand-new, and we spent the money to make it nice. Oh, that reminds me, Linda, you might want to have someone come out and look at this retaining wall. It's a little…crumbly."

"You're always so full of interesting ideas, Molly," Linda said stiffly.

"I mean, I'm not a structural engineer or anything, I just...oh goodness, look at the time." I checked my wrist (a symbolic gesture, as I wasn't wearing a watch). "I have to get back home. Thank you so much for all your organizing and leadership, Linda. Okay, see you around."

I cut through the yard and speed walked straight home, without saying goodbye to Harriet or anyone else. Retired or not, I was still a little afraid of Linda Wilson from the Student Retention Office.

CHAPTER THIRTY-SEVEN

I DON'T KNOW WHAT WOKE ME UP AT TWO IN THE MORNING. Maybe it was the smoky smell. Or the glow outside my window, too early and too orange to be sunrise.

I grabbed my phone and ran out onto the lanai, around to the corner where I had a view of the rental house. Orange light flickered behind the pebbled glass jalousies. After what seemed like minutes of fumbling, I managed to dial 9-1-1.

While I was panic-shouting at the dispatcher I ran back through my bedroom and into to the living room where Emma was sleeping. I shook her awake. We both went and pounded on the guest room door to wake Pat.

We had a fire extinguisher in the pantry. I finally found it on the floor, lying sideways behind a stack of toilet paper.

By the time the three of us got outside, the rental unit was engulfed in flames and the air smelled like a rained-on campfire. The little fire extinguisher wouldn't have helped, even if we could safely get close enough to use it. The blaze lit up the lawn and the cemetery. We could hear the sirens coming up the short drive from downtown.

The yellow fire truck pulled up and firefighters jumped

out. I wanted to watch them but a tap on the shoulder distracted me. Detective Medeiros was standing behind me.

"Professor. You got a minute?"

I realized I was standing out on the street wearing nothing but my fleece bathrobe. The grass was wet and cold. I thought of squirmy creatures under my bare feet.

"Of course," I said. "Should we go inside?"

Medeiros shook his head.

"Your house might've been targeted as well. Safest not to go back in for now."

"Targeted?" I repeated. "Me?"

I'd like you to come down to the station to make a statement."

"Can I just grab some slippers from the front porch?" Medeiros glanced at my bare feet and nodded. I dashed up and grabbed a pair of Donnie's slippers, or flip-flops as they're called outside of Hawaii. They were ugly blue plastic and way too big for me. They made loud comical slapping noises when I walked. But at least I wasn't going to the police station in bare feet. My car was in the garage—also not safe, and possibly wired to blow up for all I knew—so I hopped into the back of Medeiros's big SUV for the short drive downtown.

"Where are Pat and Emma?" I asked.

"Who?"

"Pat Flanagan? Emma Nakamura?"

"Oh. Don't know," he said.

For a wonder, Medeiros didn't treat me like a suspect. Instead of the bare, uncomfortable interview room (which I was familiar with by now, unfortunately), he let me sit in a chair in his office like a regular visitor. Wearing a fuzzy bathrobe and my husband's giant slippers, but still.

"First thing, Professor, you got any idea who did this?"

"No. Believe me, this was a surprise. Although now I think of it, Linda Wilson, the head of my homeowners' association, had a grudge against me. I think *she* wanted the celebrity renters and resented our getting them first."

When I said it out loud, it sounded silly. Linda Wilson was spiteful and underhanded, but a literal arsonist? Well, maybe, but I couldn't prove it.

"You heard of Justice for Jandie?" Medeiros asked.

"No. You mean, justice for Jandie Brand?"

"Yeah. It's a trending hashtag. Might be her fans, might be someone who got a beef with the current prosecutor, might be people with too much time on their hands. Or could be something else. You never heard of it?"

"No. I try to avoid social media. For my own peace of mind." I pulled my robe tight around me. Why did they have to keep it so cold in the police station? "Why would these people burn our house down? What would it accomplish?"

"We think it may have to do with your tenant Edward Ladd."

"What about Kaycee Kabua? Has anyone targeted her? I heard a rumor about Kaycee and Tedd Ladd conspiring together. I hope she's not a target."

"I don't know, Professor. We're trying to gather up the facts."

"I sure wish I could be more helpful. Detective, I really appreciate your letting me know all this. My experience with Mahina PD...you guys haven't always been so forthcoming."

Medeiros picked up a pen and tapped it on the desk.

"I've found it's best to be open with people. You don't tell 'em stuff, they fill in the blanks themselves. So I'm gonna tell you something else now and I want you to tell me what you know about it."

"Okay."

"Ladd says his wife is still alive," Medeiros said.

"What? But he identified her in the morgue. He said it was Jandie. Remember? When he was talking about how it was a shame, she was so beautiful, which I thought was kind of creepy, honestly. Does he think unattractive people deserve to die?"

Medeiros lifted his eyebrows and leaned back in his chair.

"How do you know what Mr. Ladd said? I don't believe we released the transcript to the public."

Whoops.

"Mr. Ladd talked to me about it," I said, which was true.

"And at the time you discussed it with him, did he seem to believe the deceased woman was his wife?"

"I think so? It was an uncomfortable conversation. He and I are not particularly chummy."

Medeiros leaned forward and placed his elbows on his desk.

"Mr. Ladd is claiming he was mistaken. He says now the dead woman is not his wife. He says the whole thing was a publicity stunt that got out of hand."

"Can't you do DNA tests or something?"

"Sure. DNA can tell us a lot. But it's not like on TV, where you always get a clean sample and then the lab sends you results instantly. And even when you do have results, it's not always so clear what they're telling you."

A percussive noise behind me made me turn around. It was Emma, knocking on the door frame. She wore black leggings and a red Cornell sweatshirt. Like me, she was wearing what she'd been sleeping in. But her ensemble seemed more dignified than my fuzzy bathrobe and ill-fitting slippers.

"Thought I'd find you here," Emma said. "Eh, howzit Detective."

"Professor Nakamura." Medeiros pushed his chair back from his desk.

"You done with her?" Emma asked. "I'm gonna take her home now, if can."

Medeiros held up a finger and made a phone call. He listened and nodded.

"Yeah, they swept the house. It's okay to go back in. Please let me know if you see anything out of the ordinary."

I pulled my fuzzy robe tight around me and followed Emma out to the parking lot, keeping my eyes focused on her back. I tried to ignore the loud slapping sounds of my oversized slippers. I hoped none of the characters sitting around the Mahina police station at this hour were my current or former students.

"So?" Emma said as she drove me home.

"Have you ever heard of something called Justice for Jandie?" I asked.

"Oh yeah. It's a big movement online. They want whoever killed Jandie to face the consequences. I mean, I do too. Don't you?"

"Could wanting 'Justice for Jandie' be a motive for someone setting fire to the house? To get back at Jandie's husband? Some unhinged fan who took things a little too far?"

"Nah, no way they'd burn it down. Jandie lived there. That house would be a shrine to them."

"I guess that's reassuring. But also disturbing. A *shrine*?"

By the time we were back home the sun was coming up. I fell into bed and pulled the covers tight around me, feeling I had burned through every last drop of adrenaline my body could eke out.

CHAPTER THIRTY-EIGHT

I WOKE UP WITH THE SUN SHINING RUDELY INTO MY EYES. I flung my arm over my face and groped at the night table with my free hand until I found my phone.

According to the clock on my lock screen, it was already Sunday afternoon.

I showered, got dressed, and did my makeup. It was something I could do to feel normal, even if I wasn't going to see anyone today. Except for Pat and Emma, who were pretty much members of my household by this point. Our insurance office wasn't going to be open until tomorrow. I'd call them and deal with the fire damage first thing tomorrow morning. What should I tell Donnie? I'd put off thinking about that until tomorrow too.

Pat and Emma were at the dining table. Pat was on his phone, and Emma was reading the *County Courier*.

"You okay Molly?" Emma set down her newspaper.

"I'm fine."

I fixed myself a cup of coffee and joined them at the dining table.

"You slept through Mass," Pat said. "For shame."

"Give her a break, Pat." Emma scowled at him. "Her new

'ohana just burned down, she had to spend half the night sitting in the police station in her bathrobe, and worst of all, she had to go to a homeowners' association meeting with Linda Wilson."

"Thank you, Emma. Oh, there's one bit of good news." I sipped my coffee. "I sent out a message to my class telling them certain assignments had been identified as having been purchased from OutsourceMyHomework.com, and academic dishonesty would result in a failing grade and expulsion from the school."

"Could someone really get expelled for plagiarizing?" Pat asked.

"Technically, yes," I said, "although in reality the Student Retention Office would never allow us to expel anyone. I just wanted to scare the students into doing the right thing. Give them a chance to turn back. So I told them if anyone wanted to change their business idea, they should delete their previous submission and they could submit a different idea for their next draft."

"What a softie," Emma groused. "You gave the cheaters a free do-over."

"What am I supposed to do, Emma? I can't prove anything."

"Did anyone remove their submissions?" Pat asked.

"Yes, they did," I said. "Specifically Urine Luck, Party Pooper, Toot Sweet, and yes, 'Wee the People.' They all got taken down."

"Someone actually turned in Wee the People?" Emma asked. "After they admitted online they bought the paper from OutsourceMyHomework? What a *dummkopf*. What was it, anyway?"

"It was a design for a unisex public bathroom," I said. "It's a shame. It was actually pretty well thought out. And there was one more plan I hadn't even gotten around to grading yet. It was called Bloody Marvelous."

"What kind of product was that?" Pat asked.

"You don't want to know. Well, all my class's best business ideas just disappeared, but at least I'm not going to have any plagiarized business plans in the Senior Showcase."

"That you know of," Emma said darkly.

"Molly," Pat said, "did you learn anything from Detective Medeiros yesterday? You were down there a long time."

"Oh, yeah. He told me Ladd is now claiming the dead woman isn't Jandie after all. That's a twist, huh?"

Emma snorted.

"Ladd's an idiot if he expects anyone to believe that. He's just saying it now cause he's in trouble."

"I dunno." Pat scratched his chin. "He might be telling the truth. Molly, your coffee smells good."

"Help yourself," I said, although Pat would have gone and made himself coffee regardless.

"What are you talking about, Pat, he might be telling the truth?" Emma demanded. "We heard him identify her in the morgue, you know."

"Yeah, it was really disturbing to listen in," I said. "You know what sticks with me? The squeaking metallic sound. I don't know whether it was wheels on a dissection table, or one of those long drawers, or what, but it's the soundtrack of my nightmares now."

"Let me show you something." Pat came back to the table and set down his fresh cup of coffee. He took out his phone, navigated to a popular bookstore website, and showed us the result.

"Is that the book Jandie's husband wrote?" Emma asked. "The one we saw?"

"Uh huh," Pat said. "His memoir. It's still on preorder, but based on the ranking, sales are gonna be through the roof as soon as it's released."

"That's a shame," Emma said. "Ugh, he really called it *Rhyme and Reason?*"

"And people are buying it anyway," Pat said. "There's something else. Jandie Brand's account. Even though there haven't been any new posts in a while, for obvious reasons, her followers have more than doubled since her disappearance."

"So people have morbid curiosity," Emma said. "What else is new?"

"That's exactly it," Pat said. "Scandal sells. If it bleeds, it leads. Is it so far-fetched for a publicity-minded couple to have planned something like this?"

"Jandie would never," Emma declared. "Besides, someone died for real. There's a dead woman in the morgue. *That's* not a stunt. So who is the dead woman, and where is Jandie, if she's not dead?"

"Yeah, I haven't figured that part out," Pat said. "What did you two find out at the egg farm place in Kuewa? What was it called, Peter Pumpkin Eater?"

"Little Jack Horner's," I said.

"Oh right," Pat said. "I think Peter Pumpkin Eater would've been better."

"Jandie was there," I said. "She took a picture of their lilikoi chiffon pie and everything."

"The woman who works there told us Jandie had come in a while ago but hadn't been there recently," Emma said.

"Has your friend Howdy Howell been looking into it?" I asked. "He's talked to Jandie and her husband more than any of us have. What does he think?"

"He's been busy trying to get Kaycee out of jail," Pat said. "He hasn't really been paying attention to much else."

"Are those two a thing now? Kaycee and Howdy?" Emma asked. Pat shrugged.

"Do you know who strikes me as someone the police might want to talk to?" I said. "Mr. Henriques from next door. He came up and talked to Harriet and me yesterday at the HOA meeting. He seems weirdly obsessed with Jandie."

"Just cause he can't read social cues doesn't make him a

murderer," Pat said. "I think he's just lonely. I know how it can be."

"You are nothing like Mr. Henriques, Pat," I said. "Hey, here's a theory. Linda Wilson. She's obviously still jealous that Jandie rented from me and not from her. Maybe Linda killed my renter out of spite."

"Oh, and then she went and burned down your rental unit," Emma said. "Finish the job and get rid of any evidence. Makes sense to me."

"You two really don't like Linda, do you?" Pat said.

"It's not a matter of like or dislike," I said.

"We know what she's capable of," Emma added.

Pat sighed.

"Emma, she made you go to a half-day seminar. Let it go."

"Is anyone else hungry?" I asked. "I just realized I am."

"Little Jack Horner's is open Sundays," Pat said. "I didn't get to go with you last time."

CHAPTER THIRTY-NINE

"Pat," Emma asked, "you wanna drive all the way down to Kuewa for breakfast?"

"Emma, if you drive, I'll buy." I jumped up and took the coffee cups to the sink. "I feel like a big slug after sleeping in all morning. It'll be nice to get out of the house."

By the time we got down to Little Jack Horner's, the Sunday brunch crowd had already come and gone so we mostly had the place to ourselves. We chose a table on the shady side of the lanai. There was plenty of lilikoi chiffon pie this time, so we each got a full slice, and Emma ordered a whole frozen pie to take home.

Rainbow, the haggard dark-haired woman who had waited on us last time, remembered Emma and me. She gave us a shy hello when she brought out our pie and coffee. Pat introduced himself and began to chat easily with her. Pat claims he's an introvert, but after years of plying reluctant sources, he's learned how to get conversation flowing.

Rainbow told us she and the other waitstaff were residents of the facility next door. It was a second chance for women whose lives had gone off track, she said. They didn't allow any alcohol or drug use. Pain meds had to be over the counter only. Sometimes the women couldn't handle it and walked away. In fact, one of the other waitresses had stopped showing up to work. Fortunately, Rainbow and another girl could cover her shifts for now.

"Did Jandie Brand ever visit here?" Pat asked.

"Yeah, I heard about it. I don't really go on social media."

"I heard a rumor that Jandie's alive and well," Pat said. "Ow!"

Emma and I had both kicked him under the table.

"But they found her body," Rainbow said. "I read it in the paper."

"So many rumors get started when you have a high-profile case like this," Emma said. "I'm sure we all wish she was still alive."

Pat told Rainbow he was a reporter and gave her his card. She winked at him and tucked it into her apron pocket before going to attend to the other diners.

"Pat," I said when she'd gone, "Detective Medeiros trusted me! The theory that Jandie is still alive, that was confidential!"

"No it wasn't," Pat said. "Medeiros wouldn't have told you if he didn't want it broadcast all over Mahina."

"*I'm* not the one doing the broadcasting, *Pat*."

"Nah, he's right," Emma said. "There's a reason Medeiros told you. I think he wants to give Ladd a false sense of security, so he slips up."

"Oh, so he only confided in me because I'm a reliable blabbermouth?" I objected.

"You say it like it's a bad thing," Emma said.

"I'm gonna stop in and drop off my card with the owner," Pat said as we were walking out. "What's her name again?"

"Phoenix," Emma and I said.

"Me and Molly are gonna be in the car," Emma told him. It was a good decision. We waited in air-conditioned comfort inside Emma's tiny electric vehicle while Pat took his time chatting up the proprietor.

"Hey, isn't the Cloudforest around here?" Pat asked as he climbed into the front seat. "Wanna stop by and say hi to Mercedes Yamashiro?"

"Last time we went she wasn't there," I said.

"Did you call first?" he asked.

"I was already driving," Emma said. "Molly sprung it on me at the last minute."

Pat dialed his phone and confirmed Mercedes was in.

"Yeah, tell her Molly, Emma, and Pat are coming by," he said. "Oh, do you have birria today? Right, yes, I know what it is. The goat stew. Yeah. Can I get a family size to go?"

Mercedes Yamashiro greeted us at the front desk of the Cloudforest Bed & Breakfast, and immediately shooed us into the dining room. As soon as we were seated, one of the interns (not the one I'd talked to during our earlier visit) brought out coffee, tea, and a tray of chocolate-dipped shortbread cookies.

After we'd settled in, Mercedes swept into the small dining room of the Cloudforest Bed and Breakfast. Her violet and yellow hibiscus muumuu set off the lavender streak in her bobbed hair. I have trouble remembering people at all if I haven't seen them for a few weeks, so I am always impressed by Mercedes' memory. She asked after Donnie and the baby and told me she hoped they were enjoying Vegas. She told Emma to bring her brother Jonah down to the Cloudforest for a visit while he was on island. She said to Pat, "I hear you have a special someone in Honolulu. Congratulations, Patrick."

"Pat?" I said. "The world's biggest misanthrope? You actually are seeing someone? You found someone you can stand?"

"Babooze, how come you never told us nothing!" Emma socked him.

Pat shrugged and rubbed his upper arm where Emma had punched him.

"Like I said. A gentleman doesn't kiss and tell."

FRANKIE BOW

"Molly," Mercedes asked, "what is happening with the poor girl that was renting out your `ohana? Such a shame, yeah?"

"You been keeping up with the Jandie Brand story?" Emma asked.

Mercedes tucked her hair behind her ear, revealing a dangling gold-and-lavender-jade earring.

"Well. I had never heard of her before, but after she moved to Mahina, I thought oh, good for her, you know? Shining a light on our little island. I became a fan. And then came this terrible news."

"Did you know she stopped at Little Jack Horner's a while ago?" Emma asked.

"I did," Mercedes said. "I was thinking of inviting her to visit the Cloudforest, but I decided against it. I'm sure she gets those kinds of requests from people all the time and I didn't want to be a bother."

"I think she would have liked the Cloudforest," I said.

"Mercedes," Pat asked, "what's your take on Little Jack Horner's? You must know them."

"Oh yes, of course I do. We all know each other down here. Phoenix Desertspring has turned out to be a real standup member of the community. Some of us had our doubts at first, but she's good for Kuewa."

"Phoenix Desertspring's not her real name, though," Emma said.

"Well it might not be the name she was born with," Mercedes said, "but it's the one she goes by now. So it's her real name as far as I'm concerned."

"She has some kind of arrangement with the halfway house next door," Pat said.

"I know what people are saying," Mercedes frowned at Pat. "But she's giving those ladies a second chance, maybe a third or fourth chance. As an employer, you're taking a risk.

It's not realistic to expect people in that situation to get paid minimum wage."

"Wait a minute," I said, "Little Jack Horner's, arguably the trendiest and definitely one of the most expensive coffee shops on this side of the island, doesn't pay minimum wage?"

"Molly, those ladies get plenty problems. Who else is going to hire them? A lotta them lost their driver's license and if they work at Jack Horner's they can walk to their job next door. Anyway their expenses are subsidized with a county grant, so the residents don't have to pay much rent."

"They were supposed to install septic with all those people living there," Emma said. "All da kine goes straight into the ocean."

"Emma, I know the girls on your paddling crew are worried about the water quality. But the ocean is big, it can handle a little bit of kūkae. Where else are those poor women supposed to go? Oh Pat, I think your order's ready. I'm so glad you all stopped by."

When we got home, Emma put the lilikoi chiffon pie in the fridge, and Pat tucked his carton of goat stew into the back of the freezer. We were still full from our visit to Little Jack Horner's, plus the cookies and coffee we'd had at the Cloudforest Bed and Breakfast. It was too late for coffee and too early for wine. We sat down at the dining table anyway, out of habit.

"I like Mercedes," Pat said, "don't get me wrong. But business owners, they're a special kind of ruthless."

"Lotta my dad's friends are small-business tyrants," Emma said. "I think you can either go into business for yourself, or you can have empathy for other people, but both? No can."

"Hey, I think I want to go out and take a look at the rental unit," I said. "What's left of it. The insurance company is going to send someone by tomorrow and I feel like I should be prepared."

"Sure you want to do this?" Pat asked.

"Yeah, I'll be fine."

"We'll come with you," Emma said. She and Pat followed me outside. Even now, the campfire smell hung in the air.

"They taped off the front," Pat observed as we approached the burned-out front of the rental unit.

Mr. Henriques must have been watching for us. The moment we reached the front, he came trotting down to join us. He seemed more subdued than he had the previous evening, and his complexion was a little greenish. Which made his round head look more like a moon than ever.

"Howzit, Mr. Henriques," Emma said. "Eh, it's not as bad as I thought it was gonna be."

I had expected to find nothing but smoking rubble and was surprised to find the house mostly intact. The exterior was charred, and the front door was missing. Someone had stretched an "X" of yellow tape over the opening.

"How did this happen?" Mr. Henriques sounded indignant.

"That's what I'm hoping someone will figure out," I said. "Did you see anything, Mr. Henriques?"

"Are you going in to look at the damage?" he asked. "I'll come with you."

"I think the police tape over the door means we're not supposed to go inside," I said. "It's probably not—"

Before I could finish my sentence, Mr. Henriques ducked under the tape and was inside the house.

We found him in the dining area, staring into the fish tank that occupied the length of the kitchen counter. The fire hadn't reached this far inside. The aquarium was humming away happily. Colorful fish darted back and forth among the fronds of seaweed. Looking closer I could see tiny, pulsating jellyfish, as translucent as sandwich bags.

Emma peered into the tank.

"Looks pretty good, considering," she said.

"But it smells bad," I replied. The smoky stench was

overwhelming. I wondered how long the smell would linger. Not forever, I hoped.

"Can I take them home?" Mr. Henriques was staring into the fish tank, his slender fingers pressed lightly against the glass.

"Those belong to Mr. Ladd," I said. "I can't just give his fish away."

"But won't the insurance cover them?" Mr. Henriques didn't take his eyes off the aquarium.

"Mr. Henriques," I said, "I appreciate your offer to help, but I am not going to commit insurance fraud. I will get in touch with Mr. Ladd and see what he wants to do—"

"That's not fair!" Henriques turned to me. "He said I could take care of them when he was gone. He gave me permission!"

"Edward Ladd? He called you from jail?" I asked.

"No. It was before all of this happened. He told me if he ever has to be away for any reason, I'd be the one he trusts to take care of his aquarium. I know how to manage an aquarium. I have one of my own, you know. Did you know, Jandie was going to post a picture of my aquarium. She was. She told me. Mr. Henriques, You should be proud, that's what she told me."

"You have a saltwater fish tank too?" Emma asked.

"You guys wanna come over and see it?" Mr. Henriques asked.

"Maybe later, Mr. Henriques.," Emma said. "But thanks, ah?"

"I have to take special care of the yellow tang," he said. "They're very sensitive to heat."

"Okay, look," I said. "Mr. Henriques, I'm going to talk to my insurance people tomorrow. Maybe they'll have some ideas about what to do with the fish. Who knows what they're going to say? But right now, let's get out of here before something caves in."

CHAPTER FORTY

As soon as Emma and I got back to my house, I poured two glasses of wine, sat down at the dining table, and called Detective Medeiros. Emma sat across from me to listen in.

He picked up right away.

"Sorry to bother you on a Sunday, Detective," I said. "But you said to tell you if I saw or heard anything out of the ordinary."

"Sure. Shoot."

"I was just talking with our next-door neighbor, Mr. Henriques. He says Edward Ladd gave him permission to come in and take care of his fish."

"And then?"

"You said Ladd is now claiming his wife's disappearance was a stunt, and the body at the bottom of the cliffs wasn't really her. Well Mr. Henriques claims Mr. Ladd told him, Mr. Henriques, that he, Mr. Henriques, could take care of Ladd's fish in case Ladd has to be gone for any reason. So doesn't it sound like Mr. Ladd was planning for the possibility of going to jail?"

"I gotta be honest, Professor Barda, what you're telling me, it isn't exactly a smoking gun. Are you sure Henriques is telling you the truth? That's a nice aquarium, you know. Some real valuable aquatic life. Maybe Henriques is trying to get his hands on it."

"Yeah, I could see that."

Emma, who was listening to both sides of the conversation, shrugged. Then she got up to refill her glass.

"The thing about Jandie Brand being alive still, maybe it's true," Medeiros went on, "but if it is true, Mr. Ladd needs to tell me where his wife is. And convince me the dead woman isn't her. Eh, you're talking to your insurance tomorrow? About the fire?"

"Yes. Is there anything I should tell them?"

"Give them my contact info."

"Where's Pat?" I asked Emma when I'd hung up.

"He's in his room. I think he's taking a nap."

"We're calling it *his* room now? Well at least he's comfortable here."

An abrupt hammering on the door made us both jump.

Harriet Holmes stood on my front porch, bottle of excellent whiskey in hand.

"Our telly's out," she said. "Mind if I watch here?"

Harriet marched in without waiting for an invitation.

"Sure. Watch what?" I quietly closed the door behind her.

"Ladd's going to be on the evening news. Oh I say, Flanagan!"

Harriet's voice was so hearty, I could sense the walls vibrating. Pat stumbled into the living room, rubbing the sleep from his eyes.

"Ah, Flanagan. Always a pleasure. Ready to watch the Sunday evening news?"

Pat dropped his hand.

"The regular TV news? Why would we watch that?"

"Edward Ladd's gonna be on," Emma said.

"Apparently," I added.

"Really?" Pat was instantly alert.

"I was just talking to Detective Medeiros," I said. "I wonder why he didn't say anything about it."

"Detective Medeiros tells you what he wants you to know," Pat said. "Nothing more."

"So when's it supposed to start?" Emma asked.

"In about a minute," Harriet said. "I'll pour us drinks."

"What about Nigel?" I asked. "Did he want to join us?"

"He's working on his manuscript," she called from the kitchen above the rattle of glasses. "Been rather all he's thinking about lately. I say, Barda, you have any proper whiskey glasses?"

"I just have my Mahina stemware," I called back. "Recycled furikake glasses. I'll get some snacks. Pat or Emma, can you figure out how to get the TV working?"

"Do you not know how to turn on your own TV?" Pat asked.

"I used to, but it's been so long I don't remember now."

It took Pat and Emma a while to figure out how to tune in the local news on our living room TV. Donnie and I hadn't watched regular television since Francesca was born. Our media consumption had been nothing but educational videos for the baby. These were regularly sent by my parents and generally geared towards children five to ten years older than Francesca. We had to watch them all from beginning to end, because my mother would call at random times (with my father hovering in the background) for a report on how Francesca liked the most recent one, what exactly she liked and didn't like about it, and what exactly she had learned.

Eventually, Pat and Emma got the regular TV working and found the right station.

Edward Ladd's interview was underway. We had missed the introduction. It looked like the interview was being filmed in a bland-looking office. But I recognized the setting as the library of our local jail. Ladd showed the wear and tear of his ordeal. The rims of his eyes were red, and he looked like he'd aged a few years.

"He's had a tough time," I said. "Look at him."

"He's just sorry he got caught," Emma retorted.

"Maybe not that sorry," Pat said. "Look at the stack of books next to his left elbow. Our right, his left."

We all leaned in to read the writing on the book spines.

"Rhyme and reason," Emma read. "Oh, his stupid book."

"There's a subtitle too," Harriet pointed out. "A semi-autobiographical meditation on rationality and art. Oh I say, there's a fellow with a lot of confidence."

"Is he seriously using his wife's murder to promote his book?" I said.

"It's a good job Nigel's not here to get any ideas," Harriet said.

The interviewer was a familiar-looking man wearing an aloha shirt. A local newscaster.

"So your theory is your wife is still alive," the man said, "and perhaps staying with friends. Do you have a particular group of people in mind, and if so, have you asked them about her whereabouts?"

"We haven't been on this island too long," Ladd said, "but in the time we have spent here, Mahina has welcomed us with a great deal of aloha."

"What about the fire at your house?" the man countered. "Would you consider that an expression of aloha? Most people wouldn't."

Ladd's expression glitched like a bad TV signal.

"Did you say fire?"

"He'd no idea." Harriet leaned forward, elbows braced on her knees. "Look at his expression. He's only now learnt of it."

"Last night there was a fire at the house you shared with your wife Jandie Brand," the newscaster said.

Ladd opened his mouth and closed it again. He'd clearly been knocked off balance by the news.

"I don't know anything about it," he said. "If the fire was deliberately set, it was the act of someone vicious and mean-spirited. Jandie would never want that. In fact, as I wrote in *Rhyme and Reason,* my semi-autobiographical—"

"Listen to him, taking every opportunity to go banging on about himself," Harriet exclaimed. "Right narcissist, he is."

"Exactly," Emma said.

Ladd set the book down and turned to look directly into camera.

"Jandie, if you're out there, please come home. Please. It's...it's time."

He appeared to blink away tears, shook his head as if he were embarrassed, and stood up. The camera followed him. It caught a few other people who didn't seem to have planned to be in the shot. A lighting guy, a sound guy, and a tall man with a shock of red hair.

"Isn't that Howdy Howell?" I asked.

"Yeah, it sure is," Pat said. "He did a good job, getting in there. I didn't even know this thing was happening tonight. I guess we'll see his byline again in tomorrow's *County Courier.*"

The camera swiveled back to the anchor, who was arranging the pages of his script. He snapped to attention and improvised a wrap-up.

"Poor Howdy," Emma said.

"Poor Howdy?" Pat said. "He's getting a great scoop."

"Pat, his girlfriend's in jail," Emma said. "And those rumors about her and this guy? Ladd? if I was Howdy, I'd be sick to my stomach thinking about my girlfriend with that... soulless stick of beef jerky."

"Okay, but hear me out," Pat said. "Wouldn't a beef jerky stick *with* a soul be even worse?"

"Kaycee one hundred percent denies having any kind of affair with Ladd," I said.

"Where's the story coming from then?" Harriet asked.

"Someone in the DA's office had to figure out a motive for

Kaycee Kabua killing a woman she barely knew," Pat said. "That's what they came up with."

"It was good enough to keep her in jail apparently," I said. "Boy. I'll feel better when I find out who set the fire."

"Or maybe you'll feel worse," Emma said. "Depending on what they find out. What if you're the target? Hey, what if Linda Wilson did it?"

"Linda Wilson is a bit cross with you," Harriet said.

"She's one to talk," I said. "Getting on my case for subletting and she's doing exactly the same thing. Anyway, Linda's been 'cross' with me ever since I came to Mahina State."

"It's a Student Retention Office thing," Emma said. "They all got a huge inferiority complex. You know how people are always talking about who's the smartest person in the room? Notice how they never ask, who's the dumbest person in the room? That's cause everyone knows it's always the person from the Student Retention Office."

"Do you ever think Linda felt you two were a little condescending to her?" Pat asked. "I mean, just a guess."

Pat's phone rang.

He got up quickly and left the room. When he returned, he said,

"Wrong number."

Harriet stayed for quite a while after the broadcast ended. The four of us spent a little more time speculating about Jandie Brand's disappearance. Then Harriet, Emma, and Pat moved on to dishing our colleagues and administrators. Mindful of the need to be a responsible department chair and role model, I didn't participate. It occurred to me that with Nigel preoccupied with his publishing deadlines, Harriet might be starved for grownup social interaction. As amusing as Harriet could be, I was technically her supervisor. I didn't feel like I could let my guard down around her, the way I could with Pat and Emma. Although I did enjoy sitting quietly and soaking up all the gossip.

When the whiskey bottle was empty, Harriet bid us good night and left.

As soon as she was out the door, Pat said,

"That was Rainbow who called me. From the bakery place in Kuewa."

"Little Jack Horner's," Emma said.

"Right. She called me about the interview."

"How come she called you?" Emma asked.

"I left my card."

"Not how come she called *you*, Pat," I said. "How come she *called* you?"

"That's exactly what *I* said," Emma confirmed.

"She told me if Jandie is alive, she's not going to feel safe as long as 'that man' is running free."

"Interesting," I said. "Do you think Rainbow would've called you if she didn't think Jandie was still alive?"

"Yeah, what else does she know?" Emma said. "Did she say anything else?"

"Not really," Pat said. "She said she had to go, and she hung up."

"Maybe she's just trying to find an excuse to talk to Pat," Emma said. "I bet it gets lonely down there in Kuewa."

"Maybe she's afraid they'll just let Ladd go to avoid the bad publicity?" I said. "I mean, it wouldn't be the first time that happened around here."

"Oh yeah, I bet you're right, Molly," Emma said.

"Huh," Pat said. "Maybe I should look into this a little more."

"Be careful," I said.

"Why would I be careful?" Pat retorted. "You don't get good stories being careful."

CHAPTER FORTY-ONE

THE INSURANCE AGENT'S REPRESENTATIVE ARRIVED PROMPTLY at 9 on Monday morning. I was waiting for him by the rental's burned-out front door. As he sauntered down the sloping lawn, clipboard in hand, I realized the round-faced young man looked familiar.

"Micah?" I exclaimed. It was nice to see a familiar face. I used to feel awkward running into my former students, but by now I was used to it. College of Commerce graduates (and dropouts) have popped up at my doctor's office, my credit union, and most of the places I shop. If you don't like the idea of your former students knowing your bank balance, your wine-buying habits, or your age, weight, and current prescriptions, all I can say is don't pursue a teaching career in Mahina.

Micah closed in quickly and gave me a big hug before I knew what was happening.

"Professor Molly, good to see you! Tough break, ah? No worries, we'll get everything straightened out for you."

"Well this is a surprise," I gasped as he released me. Micah always had a high level of energy and enthusiasm, and apparently upper-body strength to match. The local practice of greeting acquaintances with hugs instead of handshakes was something I was still trying to get used to. "You're with the insurance company? I thought you were working down at the Maritime Club."

"Yeah, I'm still there, nights an' weekends. It's good tips, an' nice people. But this has benefits, and I'm using my College of Commerce degree. You still teaching at the college?"

"They haven't fired me yet."

I had intended to be humorous, but Micah simply nodded and said,

"Lucky. Okay, let's see what we got here."

Instead of walking straight in through the front door opening, he went around the left side of the house, into the carport. I followed him up the steps to the side door. It was unlocked. Micah went ahead of me into the laundry room.

"How does it look?" I immediately realized what a dumb question it was. "I mean, you can't see any damage here. The smoky smell is everywhere though."

"I'm just here to do the preliminary. Depending on what I find, I might have to call in the arson people."

"I guess that makes sense," I said.

"Anyone been in here since the fire?" Micah poised his pen over his clipboard.

"Me," I said. "I know I shouldn't have come in, but I wanted to see for myself what kind of damage there was."

"Anything of value in here that you know of?"

"There's a saltwater aquarium," I said. "It didn't look like it was affected by the fire, but I don't really know. Does the aquarium count as valuable?"

"Oh yeah," Micah said. "Aquarium fish are big business. One of our commercial clients over on the west side, pet store owner, just got hit with a five thousand dollar fine for illegally collecting aquatic life. He thought we'd cover it as a business expense. I had to tell him his policy doesn't cover illegal acts.

We do sell policies like that, you know. But the premiums are higher."

"Interesting," I said. "Should you be telling me this? About one of your clients?"

"We keep our client's details in strictest confidence," Micah said proudly. "You notice I never said the name, yeah?"

From what Micah had just told me, I could hop online and find the man's identity in five seconds. Which, I calculated, was about as long as it was going to take for the coconut wireless to be humming with the news of my own situation.

Micah and I emerged into the kitchen. I was glad to see it was tidy, with no dirty dishes or food sitting out. The aquarium was still bubbling away on the counter. Brightly-colored fish darted around the undulating green fronds. A few paces beyond the aquarium was the burned-out hole where the front door used to be. The yellow "X" of tape still held in place.

"I've never seen the tank from this side," I said. "I've only ever come in through the front door. I guess it's a creative way to separate the kitchen from the living and dining room, as long as you don't need the counter space."

"This is a nice one," Micah said. "It looks like the ones in those fancy kine Chinese restaurants in Honolulu." Micah walked around the counter to the dining room side and stopped short, his eyes fixed on the floor.

I came up behind him and saw what he was looking at: A man was sprawled face-down on the laminate floor. I recognized his palaka shirt and the combed-over black strands of hair clinging to his moon-like head.

Micah took a step back, right onto my foot, and nearly took us both down.

"Someone should check for a pulse," Micah said.

"Someone?"

We looked at each other.

I'm not particularly brave about this kind of thing, but I

happened to know Micah was even worse in these kinds of situations than I was.

"Okay. I'll do it. Excuse me." I set down my bag on one of the barstools and took out my hand mirror. I knelt down next to Mr. Henriques. His face was turned away, toward the base of the counter. I placed the mirror in front of his mouth to see whether he'd fog it. My wrist touched the side of his face.

I dropped the mirror and scooted back, knocking Micah off-balance.

"Is he alive?" Micah asked as soon as we'd both righted ourselves.

"No. He didn't fog the mirror. And he's cold."

"How long has he been...da kine?"

"Well, he was here yesterday. Alive. He was here, and alive. We should leave. No, we should call for help. Then we should..."

I turned around to see Micah was already gone. I was alone with the late Mr. Henriques.

"Don't worry, Mr. Henriques." I could barely hear my own voice over the sound of the aquarium bubbling overhead. "I'm going to call Detective Medeiros. Whoever did this to you, they won't get away with it."

I dialed Medeiros's direct number and walked out the front of the house, ducking under the tape. I found Micah leaning against the side of my house, hands braced on his knees, still panting from his short sprint across the lawn.

"I'm calling the police right now," I said. "Micah. You look...why don't you come inside and sit down?"

Micah followed me into the living room and sank down onto the couch.

I left a message on Medeiros's voice mail, hung up, and called 9-1-1. I explained the situation to the dispatcher.

"Someone is on their way," she said. "Are you okay, ma'am?"

"Me? Okay? No, not really. I was just talking to a dead body inside my burned-out house."

"I see. And was the dead body talking back, ma'am?"

"No. It was just me talking. It was poor Mr. Henriques. He was my neighbor. He—"

"Ma'am, get yourself a glass of water and try to relax. Someone will be there very soon."

Micah and I were sitting side-by-side on the couch drinking from matching glasses of tap water when Pat came strolling in.

"Oh hey, Micah. You guys waiting for the insurance company people?"

"Howzit, Mr. Flanagan," Micah said weakly.

"Call me Pat."

"Micah *is* the insurance company people," I said. "You're a claims adjuster, right?"

"Administrative assistant to the claims adjuster."

"Isn't that great? Good for you, Micah. Anyway, Pat, come sit down."

"What?"

"Sit down," I insisted. "I need to tell you something."

Pat pulled over a chair and sat.

"Mr. Henriques is over there in the rental unit," I said. "I called the police and they're on their way."

"He won't leave? I can talk to him."

"No. No, Pat, he's dead. Mr. Henriques is dead."

"Does he have a pulse?" Pat asked.

"Does who have a pulse, the man who's dead?"

"I mean, did you check for a pulse? Maybe he's just unconscious."

"He didn't fog a mirror, Pat. He's cold."

"Oh. Man, that's terrible."

We sat uncomfortably for a few moments.

"Pat, you're fidgeting. Go ahead and get up. I just didn't want to throw the news at you out of the blue."

Pat sprang up and headed to the coffee machine.

"I wonder if it has something to do with Jandie Brand," he called from the kitchen.

"I heard she faked her death, you know," Micah said.

"Oh that's right," I said, "I forgot your cousin works at the police station. What have you heard?"

"The husband is saying it was a publicity stunt gone wrong. I don't know what she needed to do that for. She's already famous."

"I imagine he'd like some publicity for his book," I said.

"Jandie's husband wrote a book?" Micah's eyes widened. "Is it about Jandie?"

"No, it's about him. What was the title of it, Pat? *I Am Very Smart*, or something."

"*Rhyme and Reason*," Pat came back holding a coffee mug. "Sorry, did you guys want coffee?"

"No thank you," I said. "We were instructed to drink water. So that's what we're doing."

"So Micah, what do you think?" Pat eased back into the chair. "Do you think Ladd's telling the truth now?"

"I don't think so," Micah said. "Cause if Jandie's alive, how come no one's seen her? And if the dead girl isn't Jandie, how come there's no missing persons report matching the girl's description?"

"Good points," Pat said.

"There's something else too," Micah said. "I'm not supposed to say nothing about it, but the husband, yeah? He says there's a reporter who can back up his story. But the police went and talked to the guy—"

"A reporter?" Pat interrupted. "Is it Howdy Howell? Red-haired guy?"

Micah shrugged.

"I dunno the name."

"Sorry for interrupting," Pat said. "Go ahead, Micah."

Micah leaned forward, his elbows on his knees.

"Here's how come I'm not supposed to tell anyone. Cause the police went and talked to the reporter, and the reporter guy told 'em Ladd's lying, but he's not gonna say anything about it in public cause he's scared of Ladd."

Pat stood up.

"I should call Howdy."

"Don't tell him what I told you," Micah pleaded. "I wasn't supposed to say nothing."

"No, I know, Micah." Pat ambled into the kitchen for a second cup of coffee. "I'm just going to check in, see how he's doing."

CHAPTER FORTY-TWO

I HEARD A KNOCK AT MY FRONT DOOR. WHEN I OPENED IT TO invite Detective Medeiros in, I saw an ambulance pulling away slowly down the street. I was relieved Medeiros hadn't made us go look at the body.

"Just a few questions for you," Medeiros motioned us to sit back down, and I realized Pat and Micah were hovering behind me. "All of you, please. Okay."

He took a notebook and pencil out of the front pocket of his aloha shirt.

"We've confirmed that the deceased appears to be Reynolds Henriques, of 31 Uakoko St," Medeiros said.

"Reynolds?" I said. "Huh. I guess I never knew his first name."

"Did Mr. Henriques have any conflict with anyone you know of?" Medeiros asked.

"Molly thought he was a little creepy," Pat said.

"Pat! I never said that. Micah, it's not true, just so you know. I always tried to be nice to Mr. Henriques."

Pat shrugged. "I'm just saying. If he made that kind of impression on you, he might've rubbed someone else the wrong way too."

Medeiros wrote something in his tiny notebook and addressed the next question to me.

"Did you notice anything out of the ordinary, as far as Mr. Henriques's behavior, or the things he was talking about? Did he seem concerned for his own safety, or was there anyone he had a conflict with?"

"I spoke to him at our homeowners' association meeting," I said.

"When was this?" Medeiros asked.

"Friday," Pat said. "Remember, Molly? You and Emma were scheming about giving me the third degree about my conversation with Howdy, and then you remembered you had to go to your meeting."

I shot Pat the stinkiest stinkeye I could muster before answering Medeiros's question.

"It seems we have a fact-checker-in-residence," I said. "How fortunate. Yes, Pat is correct, it was Friday evening. I was talking with Harriet Holmes. Mr. Henriques joined our conversation and started going on about how it was too bad Ladd wasn't going to get the death penalty, how he wasn't good enough for Jandie, and so on. He had a crush on Jandie, from what I could see. He told me he sent her flowers."

"See?" Pat said. "Creepy."

"Hm." Medeiros wrote in his tiny notebook. "Anything else you can think of?"

I couldn't think of anything to add. We all sat quietly until Micah broke the silence.

"He was next to the aquarium," Micah said. "Maybe he was looking at it when he died. An' someone snuck in through the front door behind him."

"The aquarium!" I exclaimed. "Thank you, Micah. Remember, Pat? Mr. Henriques told us Ladd had told him to take care of the aquarium in his absence."

Medeiros set down the notebook.

"If Mr. Henriques was angry at Edward Ladd, why would he agree to take care of Mr. Ladd's aquarium?"

"Well he wasn't angry at the fish," I said. "I think he saw it as more of a privilege than a chore. But assuming Mr. Henriques is…was telling the truth, why did Ladd plan for someone to watch his fish in the first place?"

Medeiros wrote something in his notebook, tucked it back into his shirt pocket, and pulled out a folded piece of paper.

"Here, let me show you something." Medeiros unfolded the paper and handed it to me. It was a photocopy of the back of a postcard.

I'll be there tonight. Don't keep me waiting.

"This handwriting look familiar to anyone?" Medeiros asked.

We passed the paper around and examined it in turn, but none of us recognized the writing. The letters were printed, not cursive, and not particularly distinctive.

I went to my file cabinet and pulled out the rental contract. The only handwriting of Ladd's was his signature, which looked like a tangle of thread. I handed it to Medeiros so he could take a closer look.

"That's the only sample of his writing I have. Sorry."

"Don't you have an autographed book?" Pat said.

"Shoot, why didn't I think of that? I do. Good thinking, Pat."

I pulled the book down and opened the yellowed pages to the inscription on the front. I set the photocopied note next to it.

To Amelia, the inscription read. *Always Play it Safe.* Followed by "Tedd" Ladd's scribbly signature.

"He misspelled your name," Pat was peering over my shoulder. "Why is it so hard to write Amalia?"

"I was at the bookstore with a whole bunch of people waiting behind me in line. I didn't want to make a fuss."

"Why didn't you just tell him to write Molly?" Pat asked.

"Because people misspell Molly too. Doesn't matter. Do these two samples look like the same handwriting to anyone?"

"No," Pat said.

"Nuh-uh," Micah said.

"May I borrow this?" Medeiros asked.

"This book has sentimental value," I said. "And the pages have gotten kind of crumbly. If you don't mind, I'll take a picture of the inscription and email it to you."

Micah insisted on returning to work. He wouldn't hear of going home and resting. I was sure the insurance company would have given him the day off given the circumstances, but he seemed eager to get back (and, I assumed, tell everyone what he'd seen).

When Micah and Detective Medeiros had left, I stood up and stretched.

"So I'm already late to the Gen Ed committee meeting," I told Pat. "I need to get going. If you see Emma can you tell her what happened?"

Emma called me that afternoon when I was driving home.

"I'm coming over," she said. "You want me to bring a pizza?"

"If you want pizza. I do have food, though."

"Not in the mood for chicken katsu and chow mein again, no offense to Donnie's Drive-Inn. You like pepperoni and sausage?"

"Yes. Extra cheese too please if you don't mind."

CHAPTER FORTY-THREE

"WOW, POOR MR. HENRIQUES." EMMA LIFTED A SLICE OF
pizza onto her plate. "So you think Ladd had him killed?"

"What's Ladd's motive?" Pat asked. "It'd be kinda stupid
of him to arrange the hit for when he's in jail but get the guy
killed right inside his own house where anyone could find it."

"Maybe he knows something about how Ladd killed
Jandie," Emma said. "You know how nosy Mr. Henriques was.
I bet he saw something he shouldn't have."

"That could've been one of us," I said. "We all went
poking around in there. Harriet and Nigel too, come to think
of it."

"Maybe it was one of Jandie's crazy fans," Pat said.
"Could be they thought Henriques was Ladd. Although they
don't look much alike."

"Pat," Emma said, "Jandie's husband is so nondescript,
Molly didn't even recognize him even though he'd signed a
book for her in person."

"It was twenty years ago," I said. "He still had some hair.
But yeah, fair point."

"Now, let's talk about this call I got from our friend

Rainbow," Pat said. "About how Jandie, if she were alive, wouldn't feel safe until Ladd was behind bars."

"Maybe Rainbow thinks Jandie's husband killed her, and she wants to make sure he's punished for it," Emma said. "It's a reasonable position to take."

"Except it's not a campaign," Pat said. "She only called me. I got ahold of Howdy and he said he hadn't heard from her."

"Well you went out of your way to go down to Kuewa and leave her your card," I said. "Did Howdy do that?"

"Do you remember the phone call?" Emma asked.

Pat leaned back, folded his arms, and closed his eyes.

"It was after Ladd came on the evening news," he said. "My phone rang. I left the room and answered it. It was Rainbow from Little Jack Horner's. I hope it's okay to call you, she said. You left me your card. Yeah, great to hear from you, I said. She sounded nervous and I wanted to make her feel comfortable. Then she said, I'm not saying Jandie's still alive or anything, but if she is, she's not gonna show her face until that man's behind bars for good."

Pat opened his eyes and helped himself to another slice of pizza.

"Call her back," Emma urged Pat.

"I don't know. I'm not sure I trust her story."

"Why not?" I asked.

"I'm not sure she's reliable. I mean, you know."

"Cause she's from the halfway house?" Emma said. "What, you think she's not trustworthy cause she made some bad decisions in life? It's only the right kind of people who have a monopoly on the truth? What kind of elitist are you anyway, Pat?"

Pat grumbled about Emma knowing how to push his buttons, but he pulled out his phone and dialed. He listened, introduced himself, and listened some more.

"We're at Molly's house," he said. "No, not her. The other

one. The one who sent her water glass back because she thought it looked dirty. Yeah. Yeah, I know."

He looked at me.

"Molly, she wants to talk to you."

I took Pat's phone and put it to my ear.

"This is Molly," I said. "Look, sorry about the glass, I didn't realize it was part of the design—"

"You got a good internet connection where you are?" Rainbow asked.

"I think so."

"I'm gonna give you a link," she said. "You got something to write with?"

I frantically pantomimed writing. Pat handed me a pen and folded down the pizza box so I could write on it.

I was going to repeat the website address back to her to ensure I got it right, but she'd already hung up.

CHAPTER FORTY-FOUR

THE NEXT MORNING, I MADE A PERSONAL TRIP TO THE MAHINA police station to see Detective Medeiros. He was skeptical. At first, he didn't even want to watch the video I'd downloaded. But when I finished playing it for him, he demanded to see it again. He told me he'd handle it from there.

By that evening, Detective Medeiros had arranged a press conference. The local evening news was there, represented by a single cameraman. The print press was there as well, in the form of Pat Flanagan and Howdy Howell. The conference took place in the Mahina PD main meeting room. A few uniformed police officers hung out in the back, watching.

Detective Medeiros didn't want Emma and me in the room, but he couldn't stop us from lurking outside in the hallway. The wooden double doors had glass windows, crisscrossed with black wire in a diamond pattern. The wire may have reinforced the glass but didn't affect the visibility. The doors weren't soundproofed either, fortunately for us.

Medeiros loomed behind a tiny podium at the front of the room.

"I'm here tonight," he said, "to share with you a development in the disappearance of Jandie Brand, a new resident of our island. Ms. Brand went missing on March fifteenth. Tonight, we have new evidence that may shed light on the situation."

Pat and Howdy Howell stood side by side against the wall. Pat typed on his phone while Howdy scribbled in a steno pad.

Medeiros stepped away from the podium and a television monitor mounted on the wall behind him flickered to life.

The video showed a darkened bedroom, as cramped as a monk's cell. The image was tall and narrow, as if it were being filmed from inside a closet or through a partly-open door. Something that looked like a heap of blankets lay on the narrow bed. The camera zoomed in and out and focused near the top of the pile of blankets. The image snapped into focus, showing a tangle of dark hair protruding from the blankets.

We heard a hammering noise, and then a man's slurred voice.

"Jandie? Jandie, where's the light. Jandie. Talk to me."

Medeiros walked to the back of the room, toward us. He planted himself in front of the door, blocking our view. The pattern of his aloha shirt filled the window.

"Why doesn't he want us to see?" I whispered to Emma.

"Ssh, we can still hear," Emma said. "Besides, we already watched it."

"I know, but I want to see the reaction."

"Too good fer me?" the man on the video cried out. "Yrr too good fer me, 's that it?"

We heard a low-level commotion in the conference room. Voices murmuring, a chair scraping.

From memory, I knew the press conference attendees were now watching a man enter the darkened room, his back to the camera. The camera shook a little but kept its focus on him.

"Y' gonna say somethin' to me?" The man cried. "You gonna lie there an' ignore me?"

I hadn't recognized the voice right away the first time I'd

seen the video. But now, hearing it a second time, it was unmistakable.

Inside the room, it grew quiet. I knew they were watching the man in the video raising something over his head, preparing to bring it down full force onto the bed.

"Still wish you were watching?" Emma whispered to me.

"No," I said.

"You shoulda gone with me," the man on the video cried. "You had your chance!"

The rest of the soundtrack was sickening thuds, slurred swearing, and panting as Howdy Howell brought down the shovel as hard as he could, over and over, until he was exhausted.

The video ended with Howell wiping the shovel on the bedspread and walking out of the shot.

Emma and I stepped aside as the doors swung open. We watched Howdy Howell being led out of the room in handcuffs by the uniformed police officers. Howdy was not taking advantage of his right to remain silent.

"Golly, I don't get it," Howdy was objecting. "You don't really think it was me doing those awful things, do you? Guys, this is an awful misunderstanding."

"Whoever was filming, how come they didn't they stop him?" Emma said.

"So there would be two murder victims instead of one?" I replied. "If I'd been the one hiding in the closet and filming, I'm not sure I would've been brave enough to jump out and intervene. Would you?"

"Yeah, I dunno."

We watched the cameraman and the other reporters follow Howdy Howell down the hallway. Finally Detective Medeiros came out. Instead of following the crowd, he came over to Emma and me.

"Professor Nakamura. Professor Barda. You did the right thing leaving the investigation to us."

It wasn't exactly the outpouring of gratitude I thought we deserved. I was the one who had given Medeiros the video, after all. But it was probably as much appreciation as I'd ever get from Mahina PD. At least when Detective *Brian* Medeiros told me to butt out, he was tactful about it.

"What about Mr. Henriques?" I asked Medeiros. "Did Howdy kill him too?"

"No," Medeiros said. "Mr. Henriques died of heart failure. We haven't said anything publicly because we haven't been able to find any surviving family members to notify. Would you happen to know his next of kin?"

Neither of us did.

CHAPTER FORTY-FIVE

IT WAS A CLEAR, SUNNY MORNING. I WAS GETTING READY TO walk up to my office when someone knocked on the front door. I peered through the peephole and yanked the door open.

Jandie Brand stood on my front porch. Her trademark baby face looked a little less chubby than I remembered, and her sparkling black eyes had hollows underneath them. Her skin was bare, and her hair was pulled back. She was still quite pretty, but not as dressed-up as I was used to seeing her.

"You're alive," I exclaimed observantly. "Come in. Let me call in to work. I'll tell them I'm working from home this morning. No, wait, let me call Emma first. Pat?"

"Yeah?" Pat called from the kitchen.

"Can you make an extra cup of coffee? Jandie Brand is here."

I heard a ceramic mug crash onto the tile floor.

"Sorry," Pat called out. "Be right there."

Pat brought out the coffee just as someone pounded on the door.

"That's probably Emma," I said. "I'll get it."

"What was so freakin' important that I had to come over

here right now?" Emma stood defiant on my front porch, her tiny fists planted on her sturdy hips. "I gotta get this babooze to the airport."

Only then did I notice Emma's brother Jonah standing next to her.

"Hey," Jonah said to me.

"Jonah," I exclaimed. "Good to see you. Wow. You haven't changed. At all."

It was true. He even had on the same Mr. Zog's Sex Wax t-shirt I remembered him wearing into Sprezzatura.

"Postpone your flight," I said. "This is worth it. Come in."

"You're the one who was writing about my husband Eddie," Jandie was saying to Pat. She sipped her coffee. "Soon to be ex-husband, I'm happy to say. Oh, I'm gonna miss real Kona coffee."

Jandie was being polite about the coffee. She was drinking Mizuno Mart house brand, which was zero percent Kona coffee.

"Jandie," I said, "There's someone who wants to meet you."

Jandie turned around to face us. Emma opened her mouth as if to say something, and froze in place.

"This is Emma Nakamura and her brother Jonah," I said. "Emma and Jonah, Jandie Brand. Jandie, they're two of your biggest fans."

I had no idea whether Jonah had even heard of Jandie Brand, but I figured he'd go along with it.

"Hey," Jonah said to Jandie.

Emma remained as immobile as if I had just introduced her to Medusa.

Jandie jumped up and clasped Emma in a hug, which seemed to reanimate her. Jonah's hug was next, and it lasted longer.

"It's so great to meet you both," Jandie squealed. As Jandie, Jonah, and Emma took selfies together, I dragged over a chair from the living room so all five of us could all sit around the table.

"Jandie," I said, when the selfie session was done, "it's really good to see you. I'm thrilled you're alive. How are you alive? After…what we saw in the video?"

"I'll explain later," Emma whispered to her brother.

"That wasn't me on the bed. I was the one filming." Jandie held up her coffee as if to take another sip, and with the other hand held out her phone and snapped a picture of herself. "Hey, what do you think of my no-makeup look? I mean, I just escaped a deadly, life-threatening situation, I shouldn't seem too worried about filling in my eyebrows, right?"

"You look really good, Jandie," Emma said. "I like the natural aesthetic."

"Yeah," Jonah agreed.

"Oh Molly," Jandie said, "How did our house burn down?"

"I don't know," I said. "The insurance company is still investigating."

"Was it hashtag-Justice-for-Jandie?" she asked eagerly.

"The name did come up," I said.

"I bet it was Justice for Jandie. Cause they thought Eddie hurt me and they came back to punish him. Oh my fans are the best! Do you think they used those mazel tov cocktails?"

"Sure. It was probably Justice for Jandie." I didn't know, so I figured I may as well agree with her. Jandie clearly preferred that explanation and didn't seem bothered by the prospect of her adoring fans setting her house ablaze. "Do your fans know you're okay?"

"They will," she said. "But only after Howdy confesses. I'm not letting him off the hook."

"Good choice," I said. "What a horrible person he turned out to be. So Jandie, who was under the covers if it wasn't you? Was it a mannequin or something?"

"No. Where would I get a mannequin?"

"So the whole disappearing act," Emma interrupted. "Did you go along with it willingly? Or did someone make you do it?"

"It was my idea to begin with," Jandie said. "Do you know who Aimee Semple McPherson was?"

"Charismatic preacher from the 1920s," Pat said, "built the Angelus Temple in Los Angeles, founded the Foursquare Church."

"Talk about an *influencer*!" Jandie set her coffee cup down. "She had her own radio network, and millions of fans. One day, when she was at the peak of her fame, she went out swimming and didn't come back. It was a huge news story. Then one day she reappeared, and said she'd walked through the desert or something, and her shoes weren't even worn out. She made headlines all over the world. I thought, hey, I could learn something from her!"

"What could go wrong," I said.

"What *did* go wrong?" Pat asked.

"Howdy Howell, that's what. He got it into his head that the two of us were gonna run off together. As *if*."

"So where *were* you this whole time?" Emma asked. "Was it the halfway house next to Little Jack Horner's? You know we went down there a couple times. But only cause we thought you were in trouble."

"You were close," Jandie said. "I was staying in one of the tiny houses on the Little Jack Horner's property. Phoenix Desertspring set the whole thing up. At first, I didn't really trust her. She seemed like kind of a crackpot and I thought she was asking too many questions. But we were doing everything in cash, with no paper trail, so I guess she had to check us out and make sure we were gonna come through."

"Did you say *crackpot*?" I asked. "You were talking about Phoenix?"

"Yeah, I mean, what kind of person calls themselves

Phoenix? Why would you name yourself after some boring city in Arizona?"

"You paid *cash*," Pat said. "Not 'cosh', cash."

"We found a note with Jack Horner's name and number and a word that looked like 'cosh'" I explained.

"Oh," Jandie said. "That was probably something Eddie wrote. His handwriting is terrible."

"Jandie," I said. "Who, or what, was Howdy Howell attacking in that video? What was under the blanket?"

"Can you believe Howdy?" Jandie said. "The Universe was really looking out for me that night. I think Nell saved my life."

"Who's Nell?" I asked.

"My friend," Jandie said. "She was the one under the blanket."

"You filmed someone beating your friend to death with a shovel?" Pat asked.

"No, of course not!" Jandie protested. "Nell was already dead. She was one of the rehab girls."

"From next door?" Emma asked.

"Yeah. Phoenix hires them to do cleaning and baking and stuff. It teaches them life skills. Nell and Rainbow brought my meals and did my housekeeping. I was stuck inside with my phone turned off. All I had was a phone to the front desk, but I couldn't call out or anything. I talked to Nell and Rainbow every day and we kind of became friends. Anyway, Nell. She'd been doing pretty good with her treatment, but one day, some of her old friends came to visit and they all snuck off and partied. Afterward she over and said if she went back to the Center, they'd know she'd fallen off the wagon and they'd kick her out. So I told her she could sleep it off in my room. Anyway, she never woke up."

"I'm so sorry, Jandie," I said.

"I guess when you quit using, your tolerance goes down," she said. "You can't party like you used to."

"So your friend passed away in your room," Pat said. "What happened then?"

"I was about to call the front desk to ask Phoenix what I should do, and my room phone rang. It was Phoenix calling me! To tell me she saw Howdy on his way to my cabin. By that time he was being kind of a pest. I got the idea to leave Nell on the bed and cover her with a blanket. I thought Howdy was gonna come in and try to argue with me or something. I just wanted to scare him. I knew Nell wouldn't mind. She'd wanna help me out. I didn't expect Howdy to come in and...Ugh! That could've been me! Anyway after Howdy finished he started crying and ran away. I called Phoenix. She came right over. We wrapped Nell up and rolled her into the river. In a really respectful way, of course."

"Why didn't you call the police?" I asked.

Jandie looked at us blankly.

"I don't know. Phoenix said Nell would have wanted it that way. I'm sure she reported it to...whoever, I dunno. Rainbow didn't like it when she found out, but Phoenix is the boss. Actually, now that I think of it, Phoenix didn't want to tell anyone about the postcard either. Rainbow got it from the trash and snuck it to the police."

"What postcard?" Pat asked.

"It was from Howdy," Jandie said. "It said *I'll be there tonight. Don't keep me waiting.* It didn't get there till the day after anyway. Phoenix was real good at not telling anyone where I was, but I think she kinda got carried away with all the secrecy stuff."

"Phoenix is a financial partner with the rehab center next door," Pat said. "I'll bet that's why she didn't want to report the death right away. They get paid per client. The longer she can delay reporting Nell's death, the more money in their pockets."

"Well, thanks for everything," Jandie said. "Okay, I'm gonna get going before Mr. Henriques figures out I'm here."

"Jandie?" I said. "Mr. Henriques passed away."

"Oh no, that's so sad! Well, I guess he was pretty old. No offense. How did it happen?"

"They found him in your house," Pat said. "Under the fish tank."

Jandie's eyes grew wide.

"Oh, no. Did he die in the fire? Is Justice for Jandie gonna get in trouble?"

"No," I said. "No one was hurt in the fire, thank goodness. But before he passed away, Mr. Henriques said your husband asked him to watch the aquarium."

Jandie wrinkled her nose.

"I don't believe it. Eddie trusted *Mr. Henriques* with his precious fish?"

"He didn't trust you?" Pat asked.

"No! He was always telling me, don't stick your hands in there, don't touch the jellyfish, stay away from Mr. Grumpy's spines, blah blah blah."

"Mr. Grumpy's spines?" Pat said.

"Yeah, not like the spine in your back. He means like a stick that...sticks out of the fish. I call him Mr. Grumpy. He's kind of ugly, but also beautiful in his own way."

"You got a picture?" Emma asked.

Jandie scrolled through her phone and handed it to Emma.

"Here it is. Look at his expression, old Mr. Grumpy!"

Emma showed the photo around the table. A brown-and-white fish rested on the floor of the aquarium. The fish's body looked like a lump of mud. But the translucent white spines protruding from its back and fins were as delicate as lace.

"That's a stonefish," Jonah said. "They got 'em in Australia. If you step on one, it can kill you."

Jandie lit up.

"I've always wanted to go to Australia," she said.

"You surf?" Jonah asked.

Jandie dimpled at him.

"I'd love to learn."

"Should we tell someone?" I asked. "About the stonefish? Maybe Mr. Henriques reached into the tank and that's what caused his heart failure."

"He did have a habit of putting his hands where they didn't belong," Jandie said. "Anyway, I better get going. Thanks for an awesome adventure."

"Are you staying in Hawaii?" I asked Jandie.

"I don't know. I'll have to see what the future brings."

She cast a shy smile at Jonah.

"Jandie, one more thing," I said as she was hitching her purse onto her shoulder. "I used to be a big fan of your husband's, I mean soon to be ex-husband's cartoons. And then one day he just stopped drawing them and he never said why. Do you know what happened?"

"Oh, that one's easy," Jandie said with the casual air of someone tossing a lit match over her shoulder. "His wife, I mean the one before me? *She* drew the cartoons. *He* took the credit. When she got sick and died, no more cartoons. You won't find *that* in his stupid book."

CHAPTER FORTY-SIX

ONCE THEY HAD HOWDY HOWELL (NOT HIS REAL NAME, IT turns out) in custody, Mahina PD quickly matched him to a man wanted in Michigan for the murder of his wife. Her body had been found in the woods, wrapped in a blanket. It was determined that she had died from blunt force trauma. As of this writing he is serving a 30-year sentence in his home state.

Edward Ladd moved out without saying goodbye. Driving home one day, I had to pull off to the side to let a moving truck make its way down Uakoko Street. I checked the burned-out rental unit when I got home and found it empty. No aquarium, no fake plywood bed, nothing. The rent was prepaid for a few more months, so there were no hard feelings on my part.

Phoenix Desertspring, proprietor of Little Jack Horner's and employer of first resort for the residents of the sober living facility next door, was called in to testify in front of the County Council. They concluded resident deaths and departures were not always reported promptly and the facility was exceeding its occupancy limits. No one could figure out what had happened to the money that was supposed to be used to convert the cesspool to septic. But people weren't exactly beating down the doors for the chance to manage a halfway house in Kuewa, and somebody had to do it. So it was soon back to business as usual for Phoenix Desertspring and her business partner, Mercedes Yamashiro, owner of the Cloudforest Bed and Breakfast.

Kaycee Kabua was none the worse for her stint in Mahina lockup. Jandie Brand, apparently feeling a little guilty that Kaycee had been dragged into her drama, gave Kaycee a free spot on her social media feed. Kaycee was a natural. She described how Howdy Howell had tried to frame her by planting the attempted-murder weapon in her carport. But Howdy's evil plan was doomed to failure, Kaycee explained, because she would never have a bloody shovel lying around. She always kept her tools clean, to prevent transmission of plant diseases such as Rapid ʻŌhiʻa Death. And that, she concluded, is why you can depend on K.C. Landscaping for your home and small business landscaping and maintenance needs.

Pat moved quickly to investigate Jandie's claim about the true authorship of Tedd Ladd's cartoons. The culmination of Pat's research was a feature in the *Weekly*. In Pat's telling, Edward Ladd was a self-promoting impostor who had taken credit for the work of his first wife and was now trying to revive his career on the coattails of his second. The story was picked up by other outlets and went nationwide just as Ladd's book was released. *Rhyme and Reason: A Semi-Autobiographical Meditation on Rationality and Art* garnered terrible reviews and was jeered into remainder bins all over the nation.

When a particularly scathing review of his book appeared in a major national newspaper, Ladd livestreamed a sweaty tirade (he had apparently spent the past few hours drinking) against book reviewers, ex-wives, and the female sex in general. He quickly gained a small but ardent online following of disaffected young misogynists who call themselves "Tedd's Ladds" and spend a lot of time agitating for the repeal of the 19th amendment. So Ladd managed to make his way back into the spotlight after all.

Jandie Brand continued to gain followers and fame, as well as a new fiancé. Emma is happy for her brother. She remains fond of her future sister-in-law, albeit increasingly unimpressed with her intellect.

"I love 'em both," Emma will confide, after a few glasses of wine. "But no way should those two be allowed to reproduce."

When Donnie and Francesca returned from their mainland trip, Donnie was surprised to see the rental unit under construction. I hadn't mentioned the fire to him. I'd wanted him to enjoy a worry-free trip with baby Francesca. So Donnie was a little unnerved when I told him everything that had happened in his absence. He blamed himself for leaving me alone in Mahina. I tried to assure him that none of it was his fault, and in fact it was a good thing baby Francesca was thousands of miles away when all of this unfolded.

One evening, when Donnie and I were relaxing at home (as much as one can relax with a toddler in the house), Micah from the insurance company called me. After weeks of investigating the origin of the fire, the investigators had secured video from a home surveillance camera across the street. It showed a prowler, lurking around the rental unit, peering in the windows, and smoking. Something alarmed the intruder, causing her to drop her lit cigarette by the front door and flee--almost tripping over the tangled leashes of her two little Yorkshire terriers.

Mrs. Aragaki, the owner of the surveillance system, had at first been reluctant to stir up trouble by coming forward with the evidence against Linda Wilson. But when she received a notice (printed on lime-green paper) ordering her to tear up her low-maintenance gravel yard and replace it with grass, Mrs. Aragaki decided it was time to strike a blow against tyranny.

The fire was deemed to be accidental, so no criminal charges would be pursued. Linda Wilson's insurance would simply have to reimburse my insurance. Since Linda had the same home insurance company Donnie and I did, the case would be wrapped up with minimum fuss.

I hung up and told Donnie what happened. He was playing peekaboo with Francesca.

"Don't ever start smoking, baby," Donnie said to Francesca. "Smoking is bad for you. Icky!"

"Smoking!" she exclaimed.

"I bet she's not even embarrassed about burning our house down." I picked up Francesca and held her to me. "No smoking, okay?" I murmured.

"Smoking!" she yelled, pushing back from my chest. "I smoking! I smoking!"

Donnie took the baby from me and handed me a brimming glass of wine.

"Molly, it's a good thing Linda's not embarrassed. We don't want her to be upset. No more feuds. Don't you think?"

"Yeah, you're right. Speaking of landlords. Now that the renovation's wrapping up we should think about finding renters again. I'm already getting inquiries from these morbid types who want to stay in a Death House. But I don't think those are the kinds of tenants we want."

"I found out Davison's having some relationship issues," Donnie said. "He talked to me about moving back to Mahina and renting the place from us. Francesca, go give mommy a big hug."

I sank down onto the couch, not believing what I was hearing. Francesca came toddling over and I absently snatched her into my arms. My awful stepson, living right next door?

Having his sketchy friends over there partying noisily at all hours, letting his dogs tear up the lawn and poop everywhere, and no doubt conveniently forgetting to make his rent payments? I'd call Jandie and get the name of her divorce lawyer before I let that happen.

"Donnie, Davison cannot——"

"I told him no," Donnie said.

"You told him what? Donnie, you did? You told Davison no?"

The only thing Donnie and I had ever really fought about was his son Davison. And now Donnie was actually contemplating not giving Davison everything he wanted? This was a turning point.

"He's a grown man now, Molly. He and Tiffany have to be there for their son. I told Davison they need to work through whatever issues they're having. He can't keep running away from his problems, and I'm not always going to be there to bail him out. Do you think I was too harsh?"

"No! No, you're right, Donnie. Your advice sounds really sensible."

I felt a surge of affection and admiration for my wonderful husband. It had taken a few years, but he'd finally stood up to his spoiled son.

A pounding on my door interrupted us. Still holding Francesca, I ran to answer it.

Harriet and Nigel Holmes stood on the porch.

"Oh I say, Barda," Harriet exclaimed, "this is an uncharacteristically maternal look for you."

"Hullo, look at the little sprog." Nigel reached out and chucked Francesca under the chin.

"Spog!" Francesca announced. "I smoking!"

Donnie came up behind me.

"Harriet, Nigel. Would you like to come in? You have time for a glass of wine?"

"Why, Harriet," Nigel said, "Doesn't that sound absolutely—"

"Not now, pumpkin," Harriet interrupted. "Barda, there's something you need to see."

"Harriet darling, perhaps they're busy—"

"Nonsense. I think you need to see this."

CHAPTER FORTY-SEVEN

Donnie, the baby, and I followed Harriet and Nigel up the street to their house.

Or, to be precise, to where their house used to be.

"Well, Barda." Harriet sounded almost accusing. "Seems you were right all along."

"Me?" I stared at the sloping pile of rubble, dark and ominous in the twilight. "What do you mean? What happened to your house?"

"What house?" Donnie asked. "Where?"

"Dass not a house!" Francesca giggled. "Dass a rocks!"

"Rotten luck, what?" Nigel said.

"You were right about Linda Wilson, that self-important, bloviating cow," Harriet fumed. "She's a mean, cheeseparing skinflint who refuses to maintain her property to a decent standard and doesn't give a fig about people's houses sliding into graveyards when they least expect it."

"The retaining wall gave way?" I asked.

"Didn't even put up a fight. Just as you predicted, Barda."

"What did you predict, Molly?" Donnie asked.

"I'm not an expert or anything, Harriet. I was only asking

about it because it looked a little unstable to me. I mean, rocks kept breaking loose and falling down into the cemetery."

"Are you saying there was a livable house here?" Donnie asked. "I'm sorry, I haven't spent a lot of time walking around the neighborhood."

"Until just a few minutes ago," Harriet said. "The only warning was a sort of vibrating sensation underfoot. Nigel and I got out just in time."

"Did you call Linda?" I asked.

"She's not picking up," Harriet said. "We went round to knock on her door and she's not answering that either."

"We've nowhere to go," Nigel added. "I suppose we're lucky to be alive."

Donnie and I looked at each other. He gave me a nod.

"Our rental unit's just been fixed up," I said. "They've repaired the fire damage. I mean, if you don't mind that Mr. Henriques…um…"

"Why don't you come spend the night?" Donnie interrupted.

"Ah, just like old times, eh darling?" Nigel said to Harriet.

"What?" Donnie said.

"Barda, you've got a vacancy then?" Harriet said to me. "This is opportune."

"A vacancy? Yes. Yes, I guess we do."

"Okay, great," Donnie said. "I'll go get my car. We can move a few of your things down before it starts raining again. Seems a lot has happened since I've been gone."

"I'll come with and fill you in." Harriet trotted downhill to join Donnie and Francesca. "Back in two shakes."

This was terrible luck for Harriet and Nigel, but all things considered, it was a stroke of good fortune for us. We weren't likely to get better tenants than Harriet and Nigel Holmes. They were eccentric, sure, and my being Harriet's department chair was a little awkward. But they weren't going to throw noisy parties or vandalize the property. And I knew I could count on them to pay the rent.

Linda Wilson wouldn't be happy about our poaching her tenants. Too bad. She didn't maintain her property. It was a wonder no one was hurt. Linda had no one to blame but herself. Not that it would make any difference to her. She would still think of some way to blame me.

Nigel was already poking through the remnants of the collapsed house.

I went over to join him and examined the rubble to see what I could safely salvage.

"Here, let me help," I said. "I don't know what's important, but—"

"No, no, please," he insisted. "We're already causing you enough trouble."

"No trouble at all." I saw the corner of a check stub poking out of the rubble and tugged it free. "We keep new toothbrushes and spare sweats just for guests. Tomorrow's a school day, and…"

Something on the check stub caught my attention.

"OMH dot com?" I read. "Why does that sound…"

I looked up to meet Nigel's gaze. Nigel's complexion normally tended toward the florid, but in the sodium light he looked practically purple. And despite the cool evening, he was sweating.

"Silly for us to be poking about in the dark like this," he stammered. "Not sure what I was thinking, really. We might as well head over to yours, take care of this tomorrow when it's daylight."

"Nigel," I said. "OMH dot com? Is this *OutsourceMyHomework dot com*? What is this?"

Nigel gulped.

"You mustn't tell Harriet," he pleaded.

"*You* wrote those business plans for my students. It was you, wasn't it?"

FRANKIE BOW

"Well, I…"

"Party Pooper?" I demanded. "Toot Sweet? *Urine Luck*?"

"Yes, that was rather good, if I do say so—"

"You taught at Balliol College! And here you are enabling academic dishonesty! What were you thinking?"

"You don't understand, Molly." Nigel looked down at the rubble beneath his feet. "Harriet thinks I've found a publisher for my memoir."

"There are other ways to make money besides writing for an essay mill," I said. "Legal, non-scummy ways."

"It's not to do with money," Nigel said quietly. "We've got loads. It's just that Harriet is so proud of me. She'd be crushed to know the truth."

I saw the headlights of Donnie's car coming up the street.

"I won't tell Harriet," I said. "Okay? But Nigel, you have to promise me two things. First, if you're going to be renting our place, no more of this essay mill business. I'm legally liable for any criminal acts you commit on my property and the last thing I need is to get caught up in something like this. Tell Harriet you've already gotten the full amount of your advance and have that be the end of it. Don't worry about royalties. Most books don't earn out anyway."

"Fair enough." Nigel dabbed his eye with the back of his wrist. "What's the second thing?"

CHAPTER FORTY-EIGHT

THE SENIOR SHOWCASE, THE END-OF-THE YEAR EVENT WHERE
Mahina State's Friends in the Business Community came to
admire our best student work, was as scandal-free as I (and
Victor Santiago) could have hoped. The business plans on
display were an uninspired assortment of sports bars, party
planners, and online clothing stores. The miscreants who had
purchased their assignments from OutsourceMyHomework
were not represented at the Senior Showcase. I had already
assigned them failing grades for the course and reported them
to the Office of Student Conduct. There they suffered severe
consequences for their intellectual larceny, if by "severe" you
mean "gently guided into an independent-studies program
and allowed to complete their degrees by sleight of
paperwork."

Despite my class's unremarkable showing, Victor Santiago,
Vice-President for Student Outreach and Community
Relations, was in a cheerful mood. The reason? He had just
received news of an anonymous and shockingly generous
donation to the university. During the closing remarks of the
Senior Showcase, Santiago called me up to stand next to him
as he made the announcement.

Please accept this gift to the Mahina State University College of Commerce, given in appreciation for the Department of Management and its department head, Dr. Molly Barda. Her tireless devotion to academic integrity has inspired this donation. In short, she's bloody marvelous.

As I watched Victor Santiago read those words, I thought I saw him smile.

THE END

ABOUT THE AUTHOR

Frankie Bow teaches at a public university and writes licensed Miss Fortune World novellas as well as The Professor Molly Mysteries. Unlike Professor Molly, Frankie is blessed with delightful students, sane colleagues, and a perfectly nice office chair.

Thank you for taking the time to read The Influencer. If you enjoyed it, please consider telling your friends and posting a short review. Word of mouth is an author's best friend and much appreciated.
Mahalo, Frankie

www.ingramcontent.com/pod-product-compliance
Lightning Source LLC
Chambersburg PA
CBHW070857250626
47159CB00003B/1096